D0955483

Let the adventure begin...
—AW

For my Little B and my Little Bird.
—PG

Copyright © 2023 by Sourcebooks
Illustrations by Paul Gill
Cover and internal design © 2023 by Sourcebooks
Cover and internal design by Maryn Arreguín/Sourcebooks

Sourcebooks and the colophon are registered trademarks of Sourcebooks

All rights reserved.

This artwork was created in Procreate on an iPad Pro and finished in Photoshop.

Published by Sourcebooks Wonderland, an imprint of Sourcebooks Kids
P.O. Box 4410, Naperville, Illinois 60567-4410
(630) 961-3900
sourcebookskids.com

Cataloging-in-Publication Data is on file with the Library of Congress.

Source of Production: Wing King Tong Paper Products Co. Ltd., Shenzhen, Guangdong Province, China
Date of Production: February 2023
Run Number: 5029973

Printed and bound in China.
WKT 10 9 8 7 6 5 4 3 2 1

PUP and DRAGON

How to Catch an Elf

A Graphic Novel by **Alice Walstead**
Illustrations by **Paul Gill**

sourcebooks
wonderland

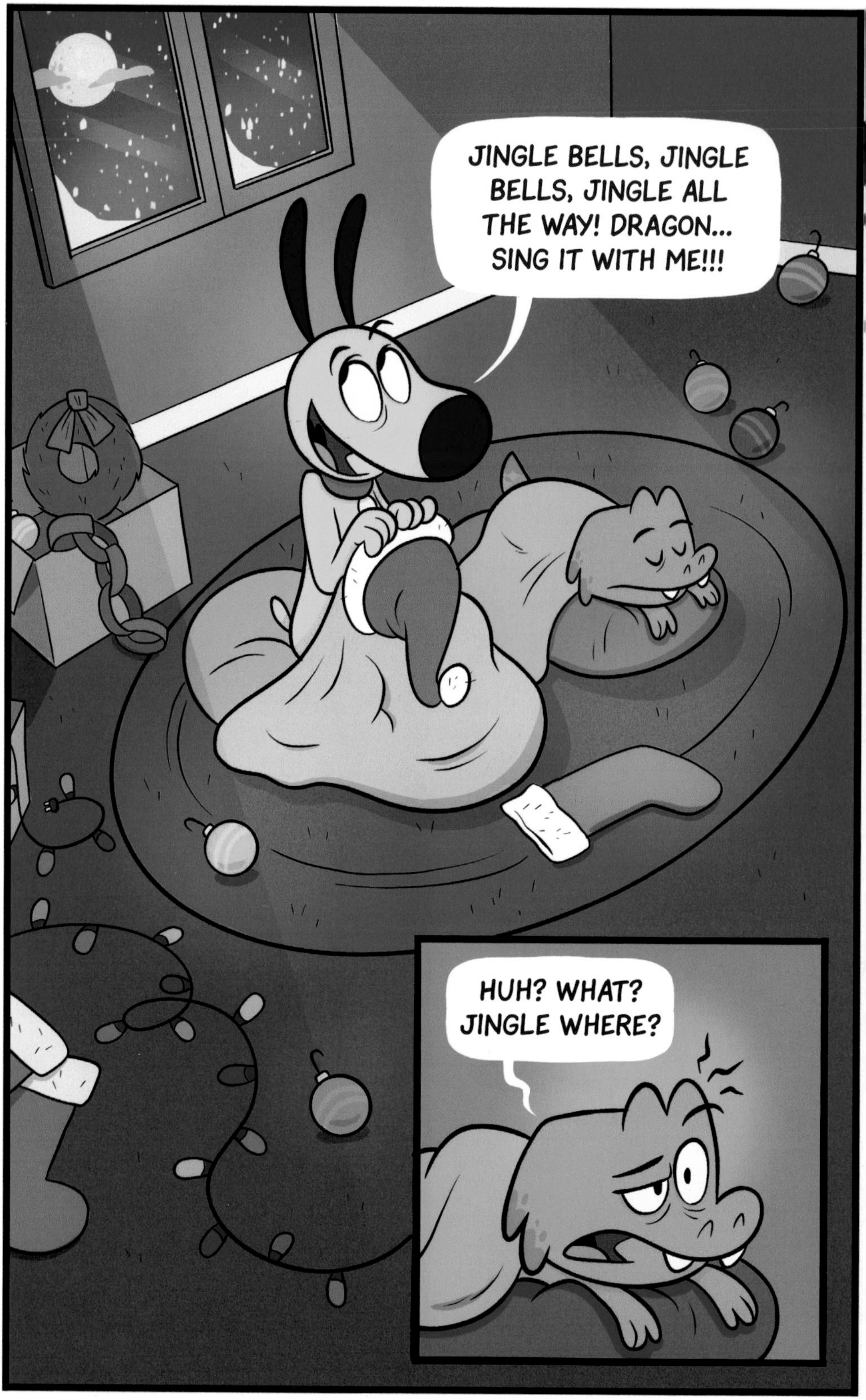
JINGLE BELLS, JINGLE BELLS, JINGLE ALL THE WAY! DRAGON... SING IT WITH ME!!!
HUH? WHAT? JINGLE WHERE?

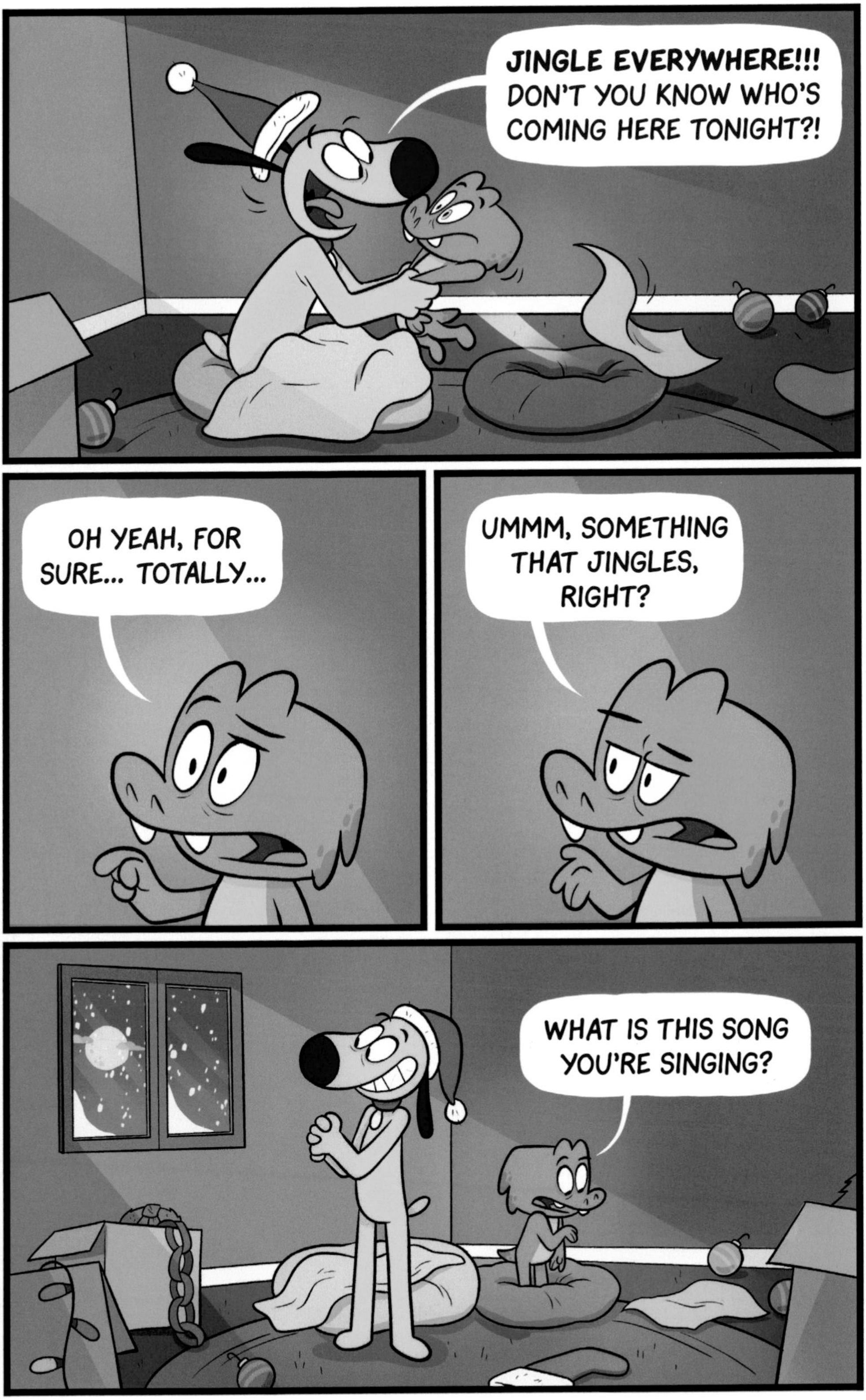
JINGLE EVERYWHERE!!! DON'T YOU KNOW WHO'S COMING HERE TONIGHT?!
OH YEAH, FOR SURE... TOTALLY...
UMMM, SOMETHING THAT JINGLES, RIGHT?
WHAT IS THIS SONG YOU'RE SINGING?

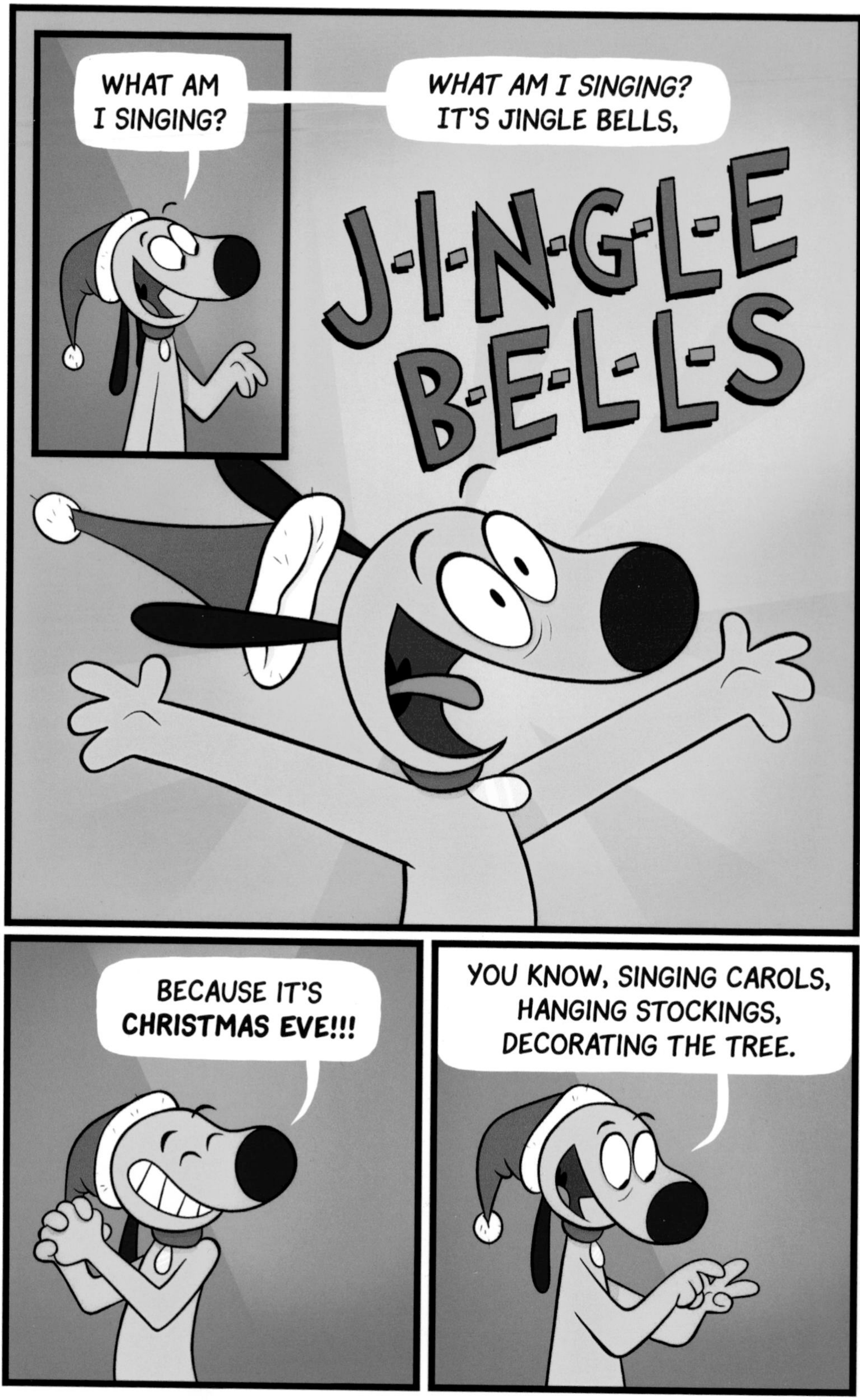
WHAT AM
I SINGING?
WHAT AM I SINGING?
IT'S JINGLE BELLS,
J-I-N-G-L-E
B-E-L-L-S
BECAUSE IT'S
CHRISTMAS EVE!!!
YOU KNOW, SINGING CAROLS,
HANGING STOCKINGS,
DECORATING THE TREE.

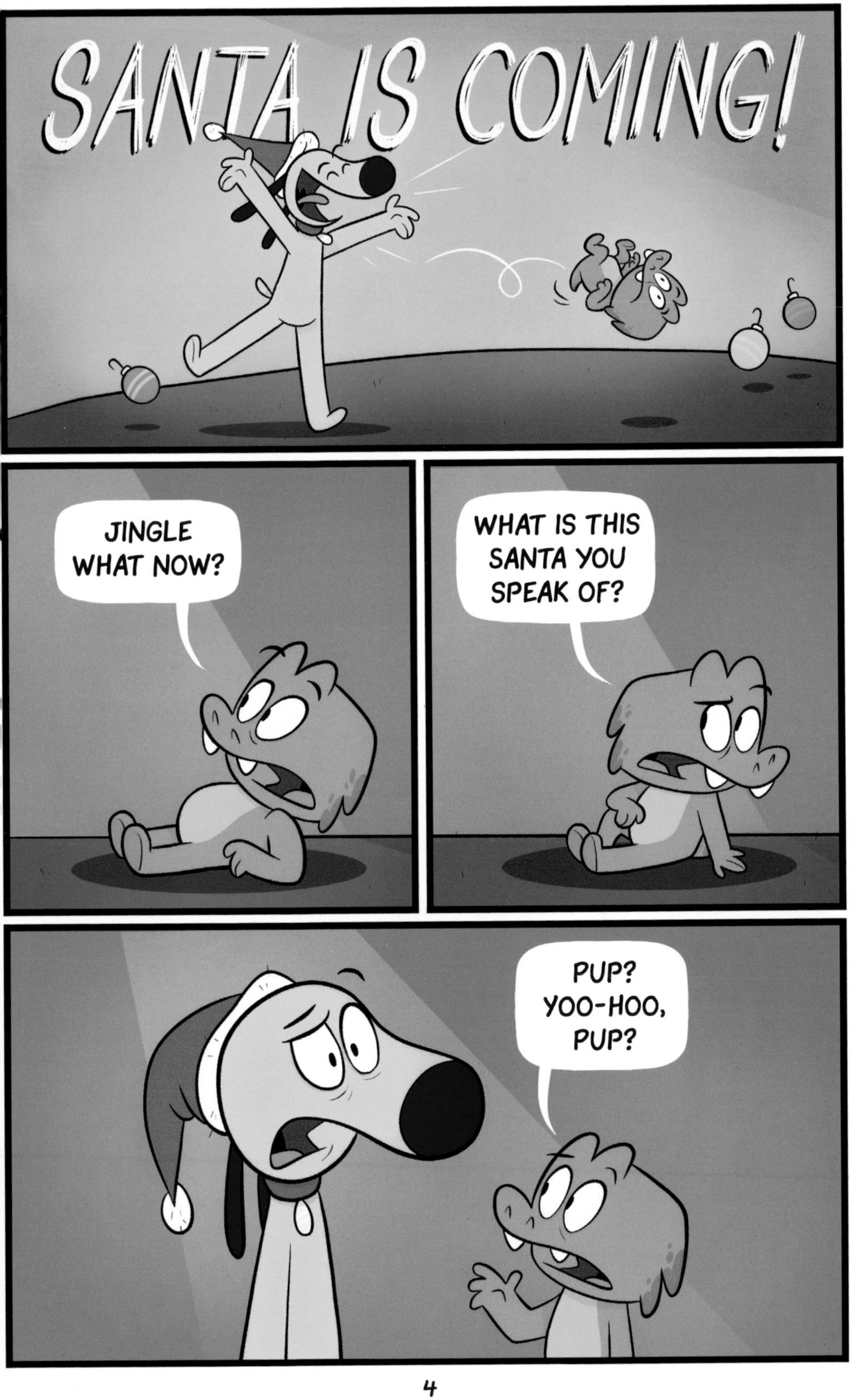
SANTA IS COMING!
JINGLE WHAT NOW?
WHAT IS THIS SANTA YOU SPEAK OF?
PUP? YOO-HOO, PUP?

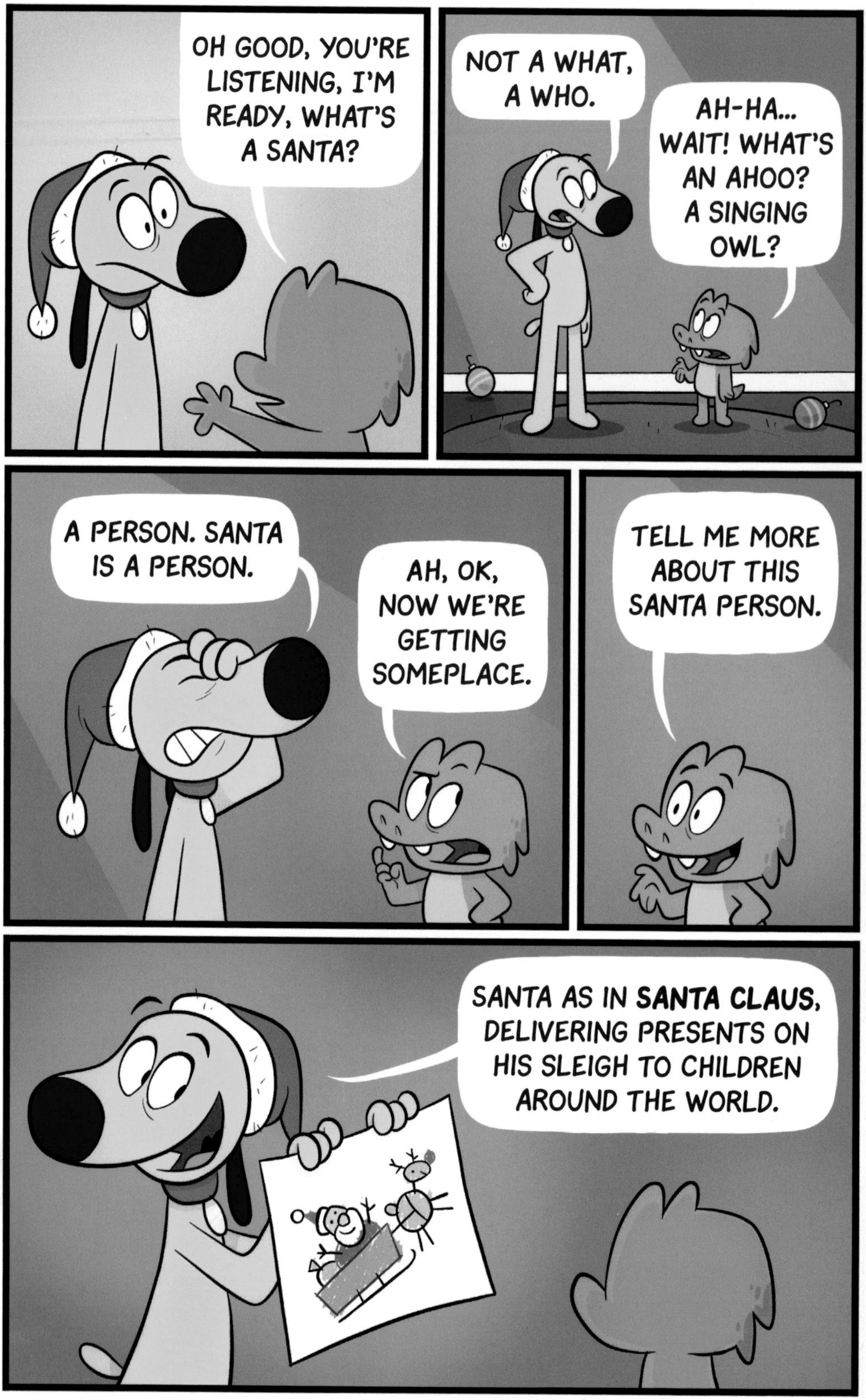
OH GOOD, YOU'RE LISTENING, I'M READY, WHAT'S A SANTA?
NOT A WHAT, A WHO.
AH-HA... WAIT! WHAT'S AN AHOO? A SINGING OWL?
A PERSON. SANTA IS A PERSON.
AH, OK, NOW WE'RE GETTING SOMEPLACE.
TELL ME MORE ABOUT THIS SANTA PERSON.
SANTA AS IN **SANTA CLAUS**, DELIVERING PRESENTS ON HIS SLEIGH TO CHILDREN AROUND THE WORLD.

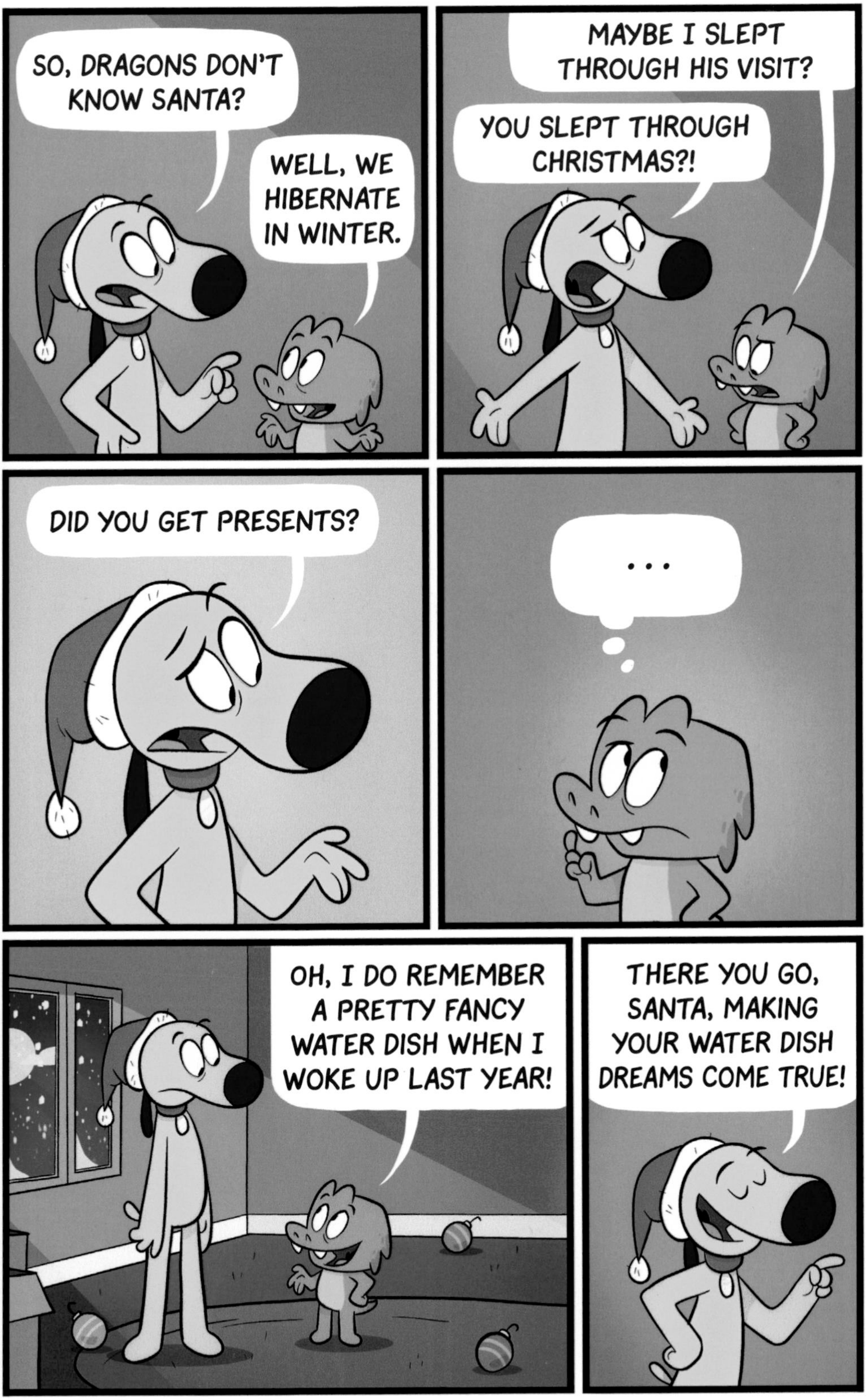
SO, DRAGONS DON'T KNOW SANTA?
WELL, WE HIBERNATE IN WINTER.
MAYBE I SLEPT THROUGH HIS VISIT?
YOU SLEPT THROUGH CHRISTMAS?!
DID YOU GET PRESENTS?
...
OH, I DO REMEMBER A PRETTY FANCY WATER DISH WHEN I WOKE UP LAST YEAR!
THERE YOU GO, SANTA, MAKING YOUR WATER DISH DREAMS COME TRUE!

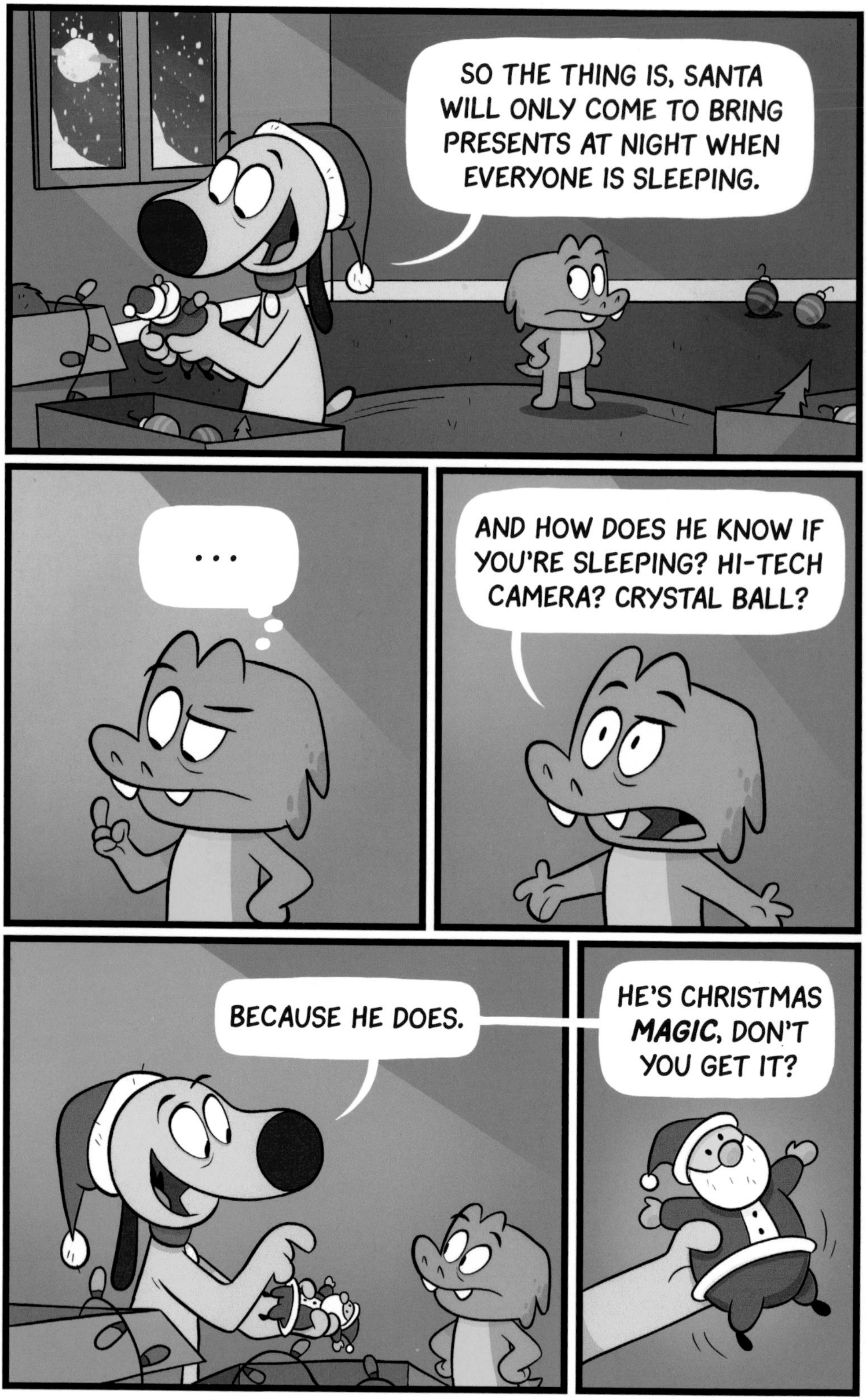
SO THE THING IS, SANTA WILL ONLY COME TO BRING PRESENTS AT NIGHT WHEN EVERYONE IS SLEEPING.
...
AND HOW DOES HE KNOW IF YOU'RE SLEEPING? HI-TECH CAMERA? CRYSTAL BALL?
BECAUSE HE DOES.
HE'S CHRISTMAS *MAGIC*, DON'T YOU GET IT?

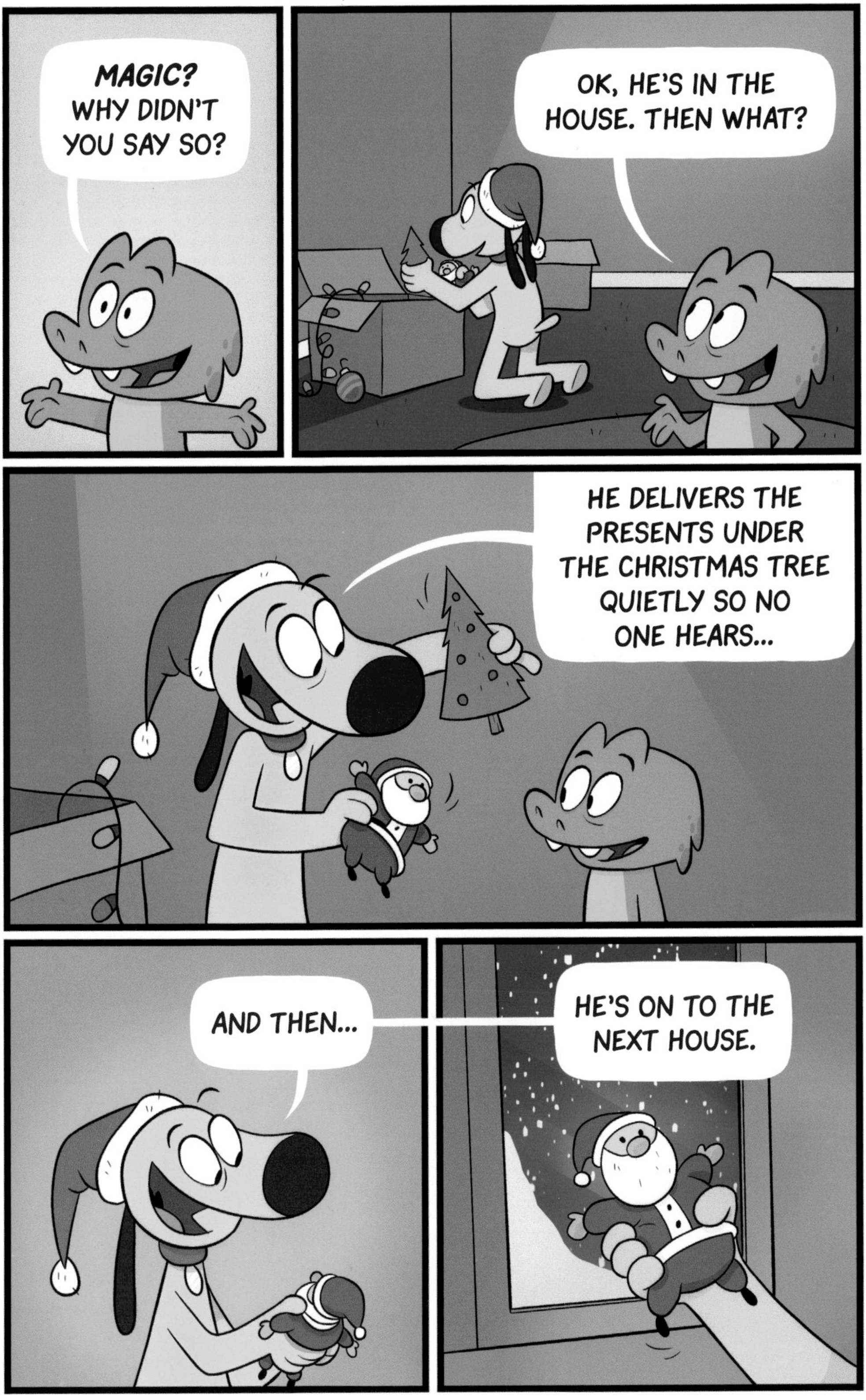
MAGIC? WHY DIDN'T YOU SAY SO?
OK, HE'S IN THE HOUSE. THEN WHAT?
HE DELIVERS THE PRESENTS UNDER THE CHRISTMAS TREE QUIETLY SO NO ONE HEARS...
AND THEN...
HE'S ON TO THE NEXT HOUSE.

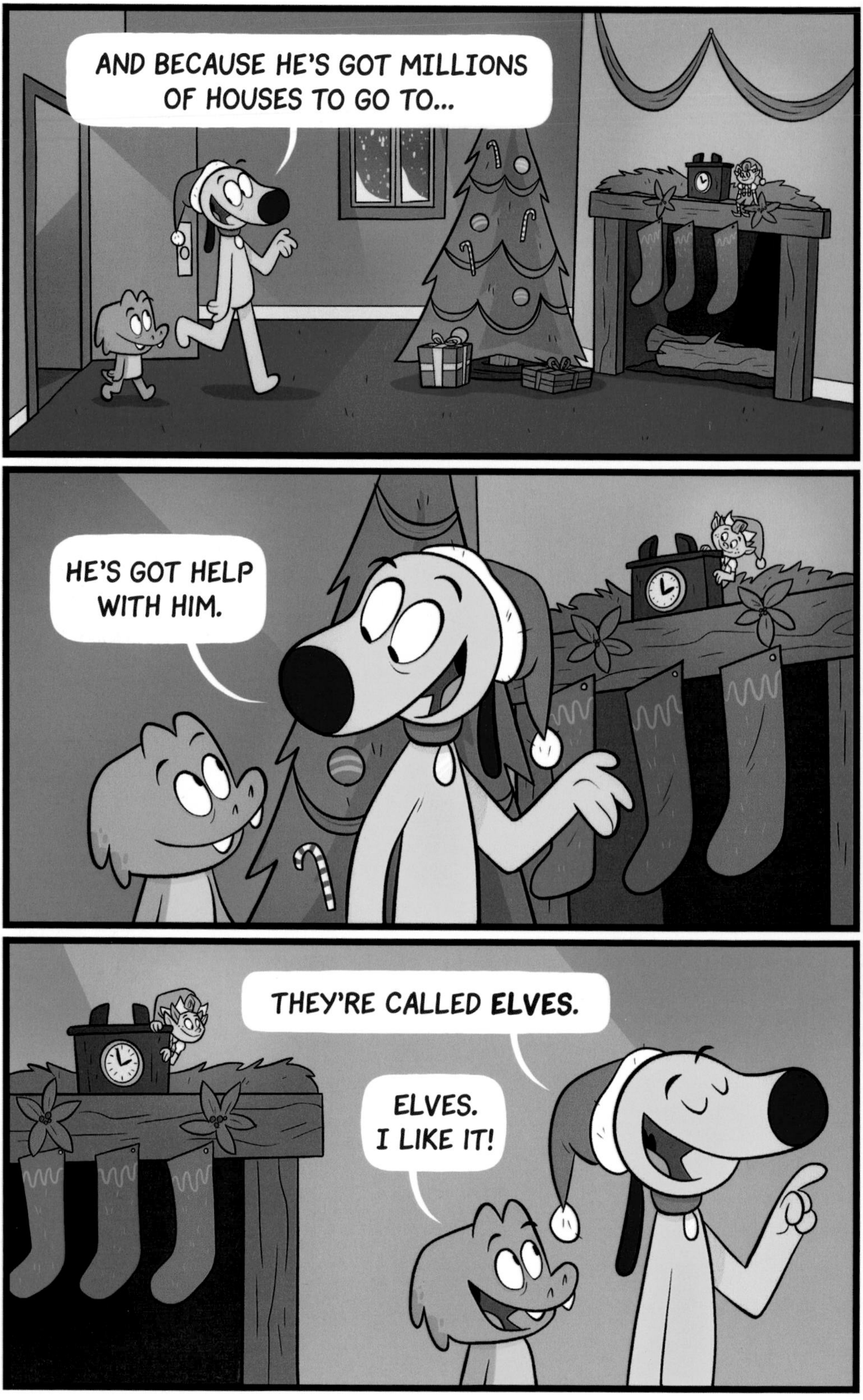
AND BECAUSE HE'S GOT MILLIONS OF HOUSES TO GO TO...
HE'S GOT HELP WITH HIM.
THEY'RE CALLED **ELVES.**
ELVES. I LIKE IT!

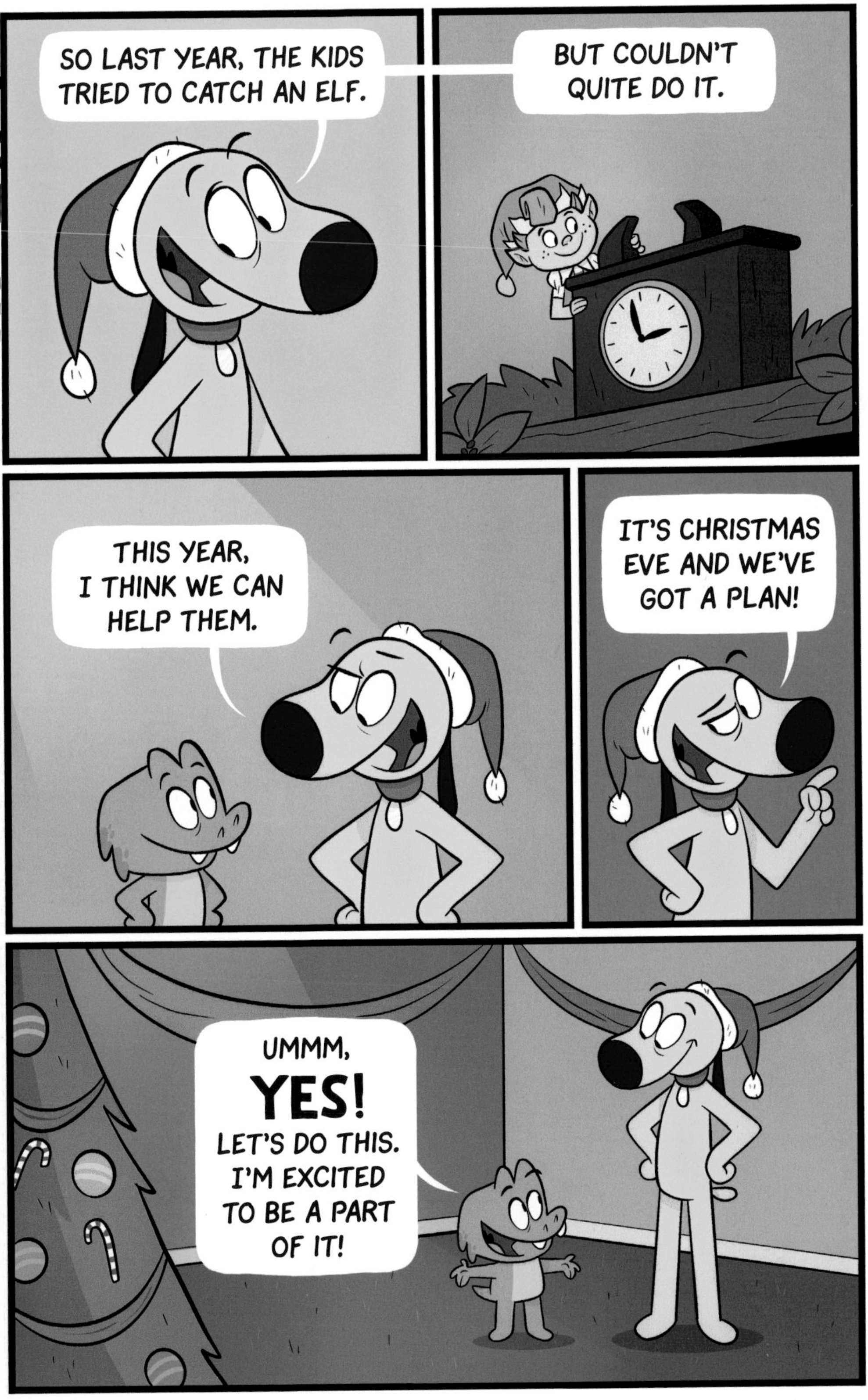
SO LAST YEAR, THE KIDS TRIED TO CATCH AN ELF.
BUT COULDN'T QUITE DO IT.
THIS YEAR, I THINK WE CAN HELP THEM.
IT'S CHRISTMAS EVE AND WE'VE GOT A PLAN!
UMMM, **YES!** LET'S DO THIS. I'M EXCITED TO BE A PART OF IT!

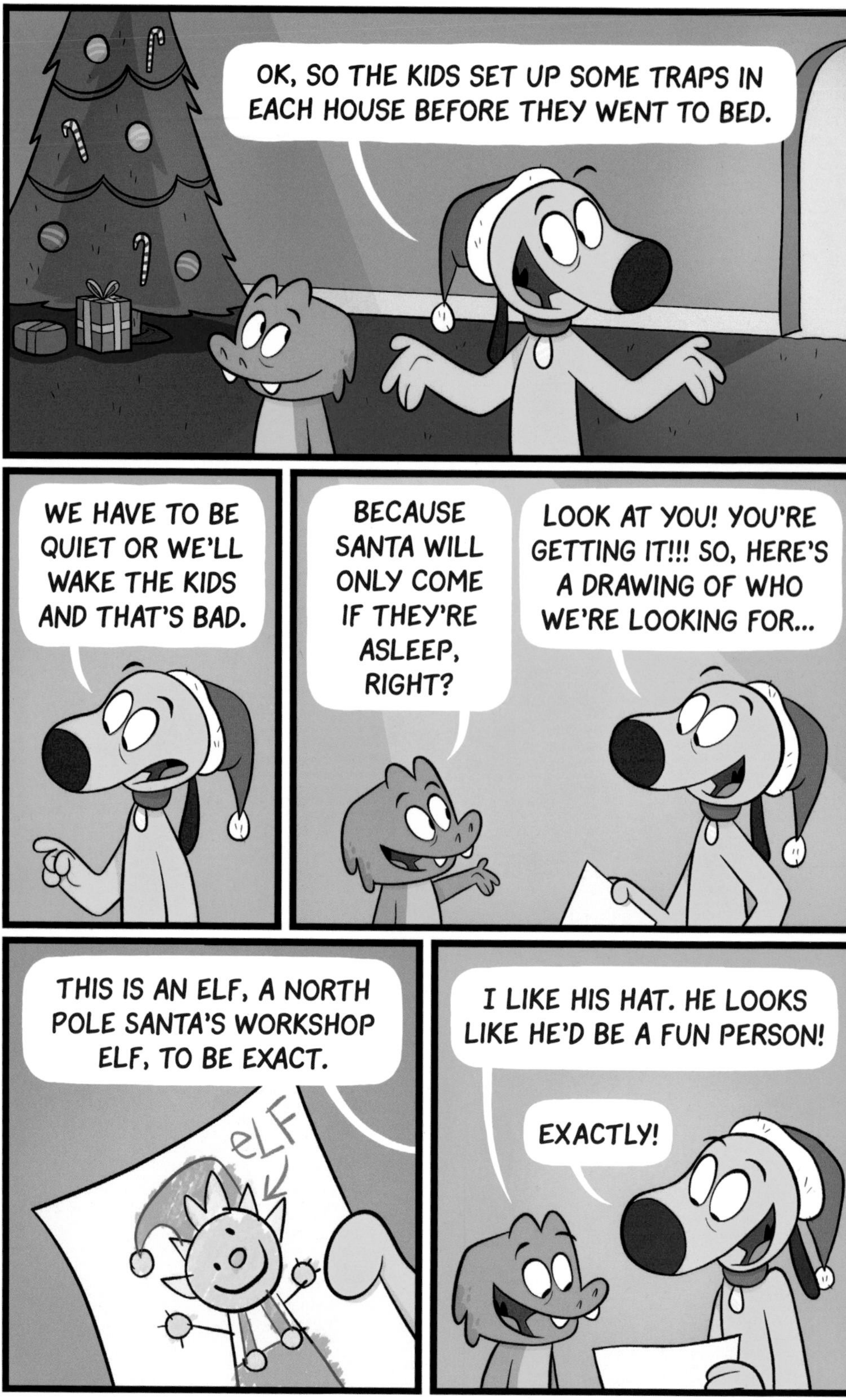

OK, SO THE KIDS SET UP SOME TRAPS IN EACH HOUSE BEFORE THEY WENT TO BED.
WE HAVE TO BE QUIET OR WE'LL WAKE THE KIDS AND THAT'S BAD.
BECAUSE SANTA WILL ONLY COME IF THEY'RE ASLEEP, RIGHT?
LOOK AT YOU! YOU'RE GETTING IT!!! SO, HERE'S A DRAWING OF WHO WE'RE LOOKING FOR...
THIS IS AN ELF, A NORTH POLE SANTA'S WORKSHOP ELF, TO BE EXACT.
eLF
I LIKE HIS HAT. HE LOOKS LIKE HE'D BE A FUN PERSON!
EXACTLY!

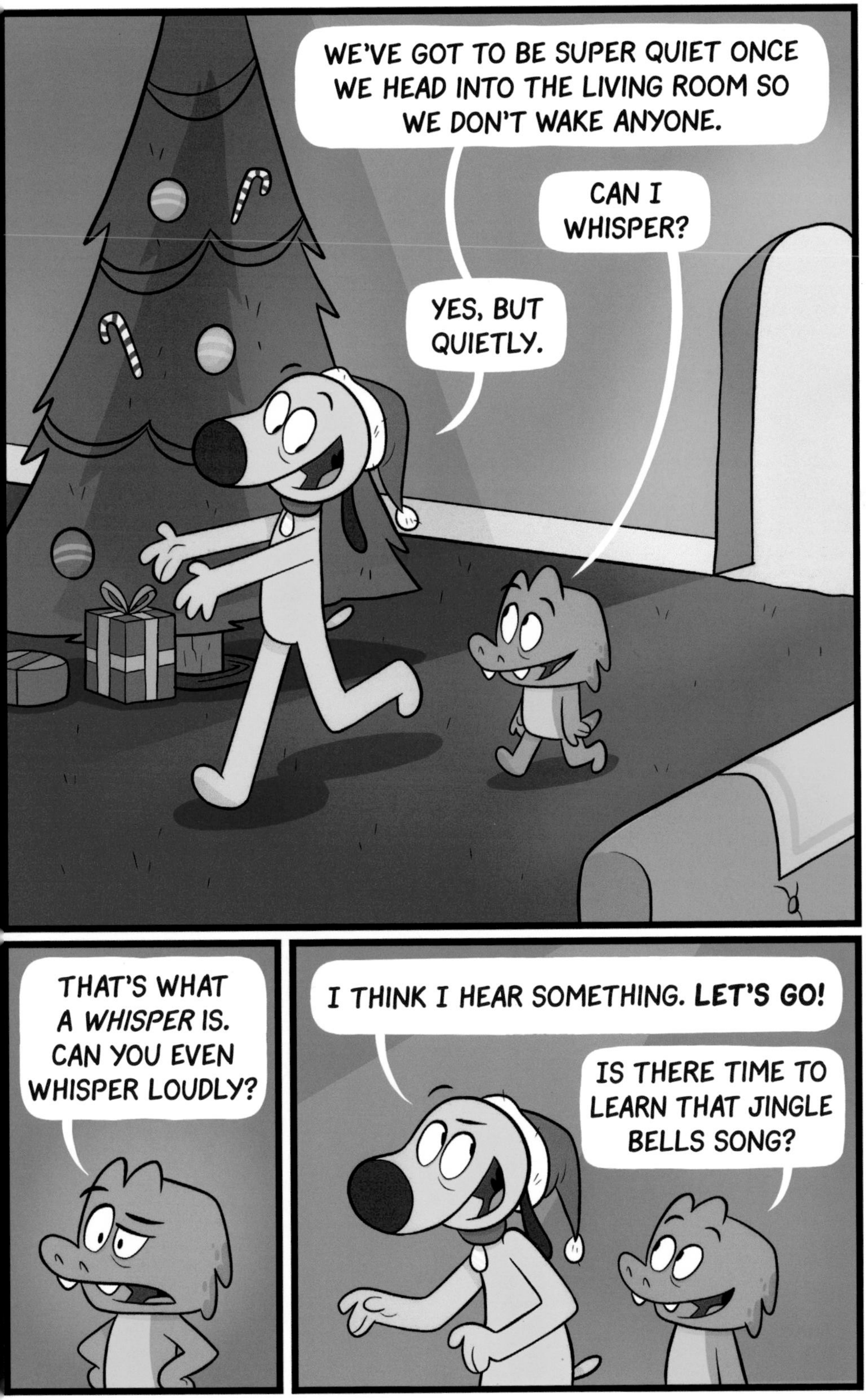
WE'VE GOT TO BE SUPER QUIET ONCE WE HEAD INTO THE LIVING ROOM SO WE DON'T WAKE ANYONE.
CAN I WHISPER?
YES, BUT QUIETLY.
THAT'S WHAT A *WHISPER* IS. CAN YOU EVEN WHISPER LOUDLY?
I THINK I HEAR SOMETHING. **LET'S GO!**
IS THERE TIME TO LEARN THAT JINGLE BELLS SONG?

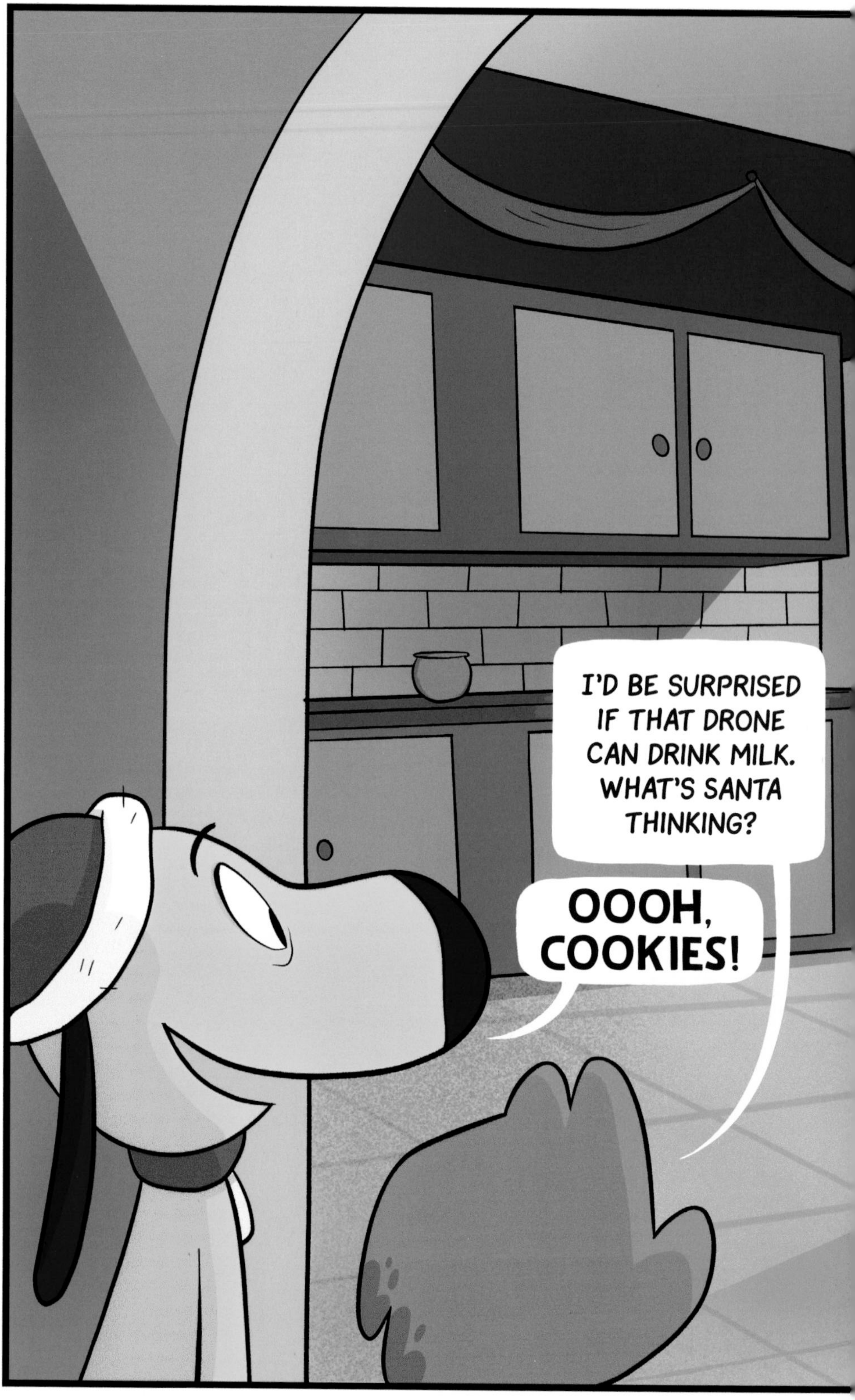
I'D BE SURPRISED IF THAT DRONE CAN DRINK MILK. WHAT'S SANTA THINKING?
OOOH, COOKIES!

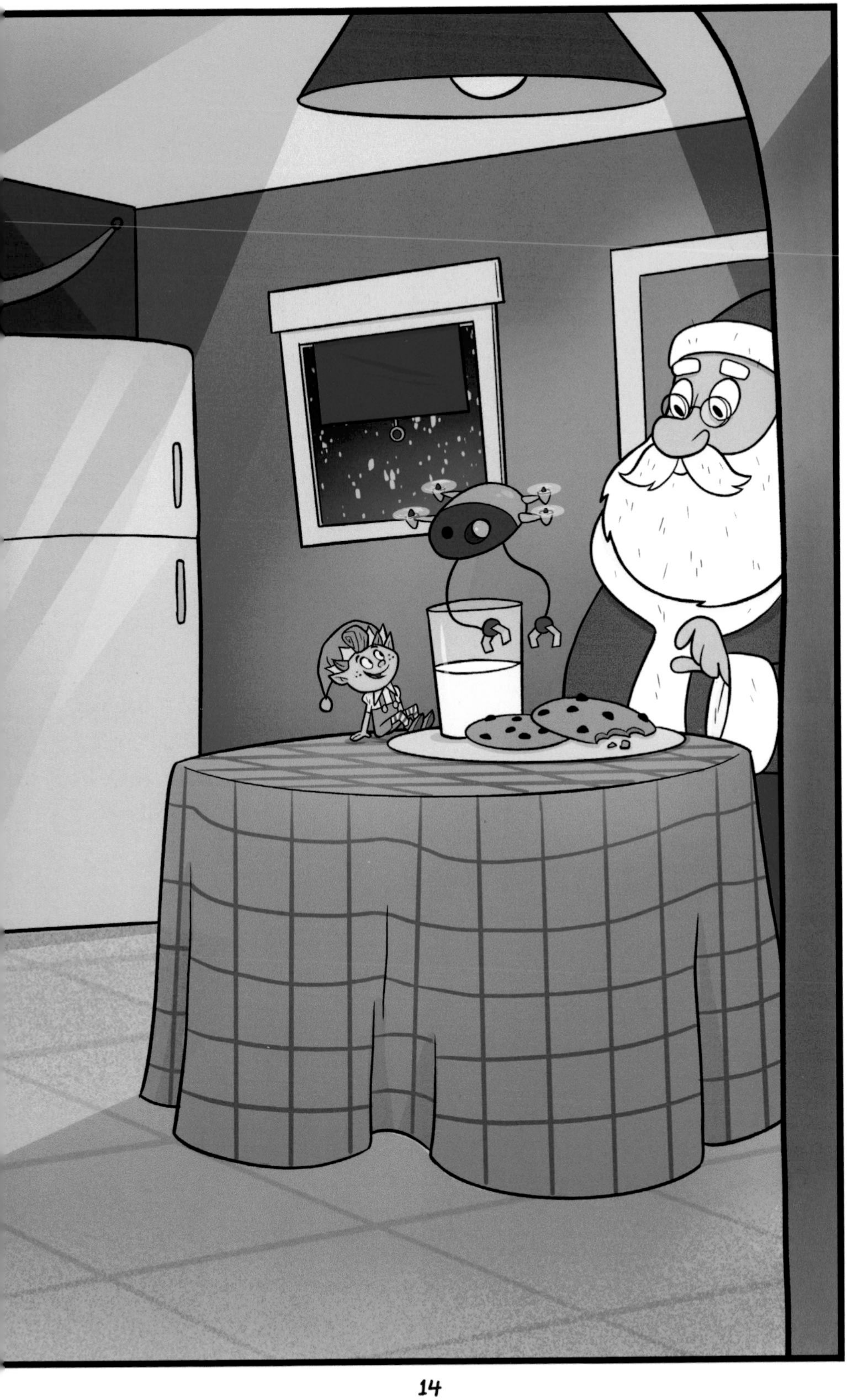

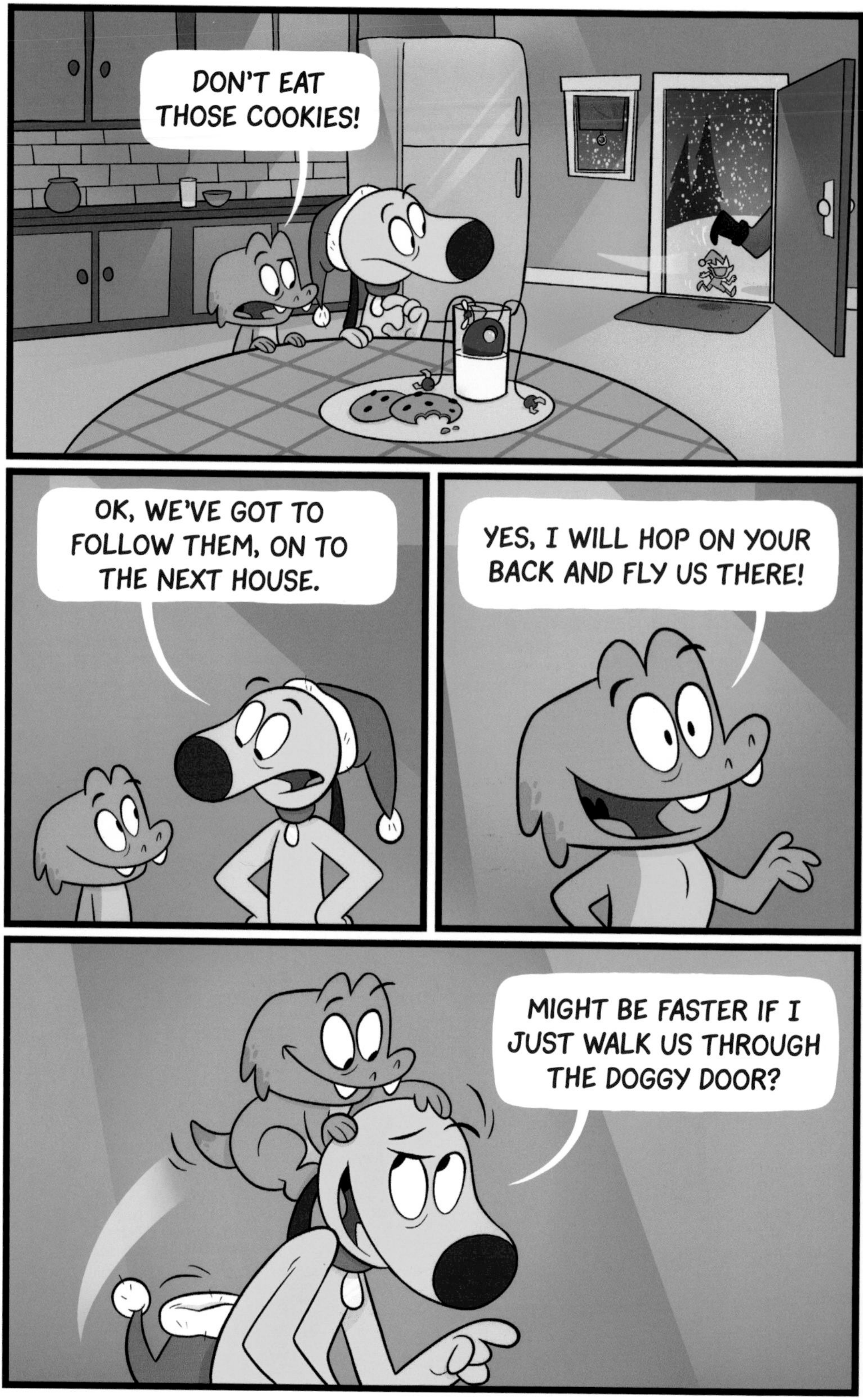
DON'T EAT THOSE COOKIES!
OK, WE'VE GOT TO FOLLOW THEM, ON TO THE NEXT HOUSE.
YES, I WILL HOP ON YOUR BACK AND FLY US THERE!
MIGHT BE FASTER IF I JUST WALK US THROUGH THE DOGGY DOOR?

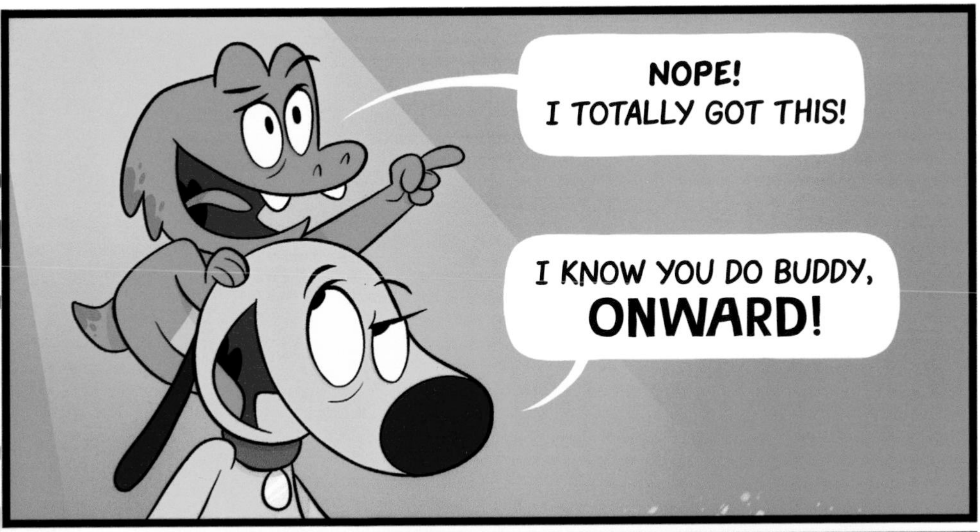
NOPE!
I TOTALLY GOT THIS!
I KNOW YOU DO BUDDY, ONWARD!

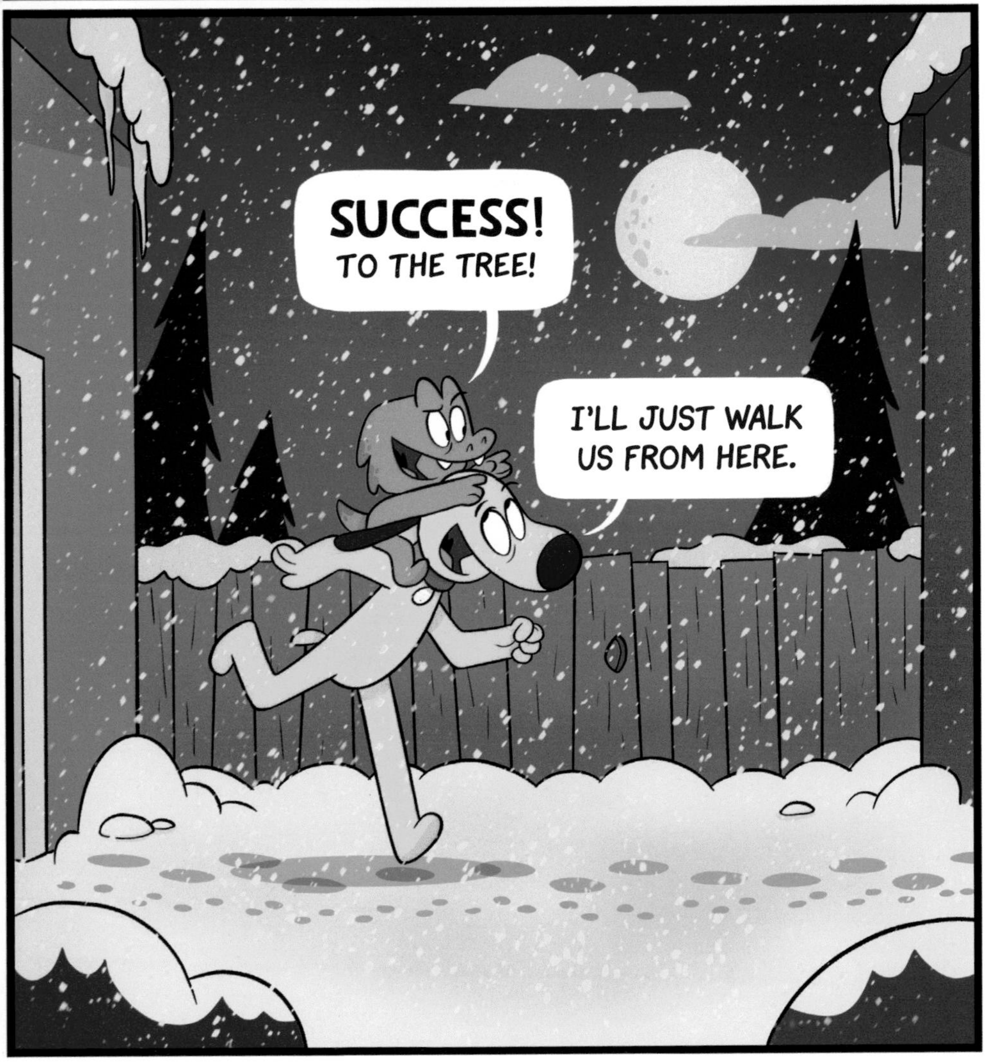
SUCCESS! TO THE TREE!
I'LL JUST WALK US FROM HERE.

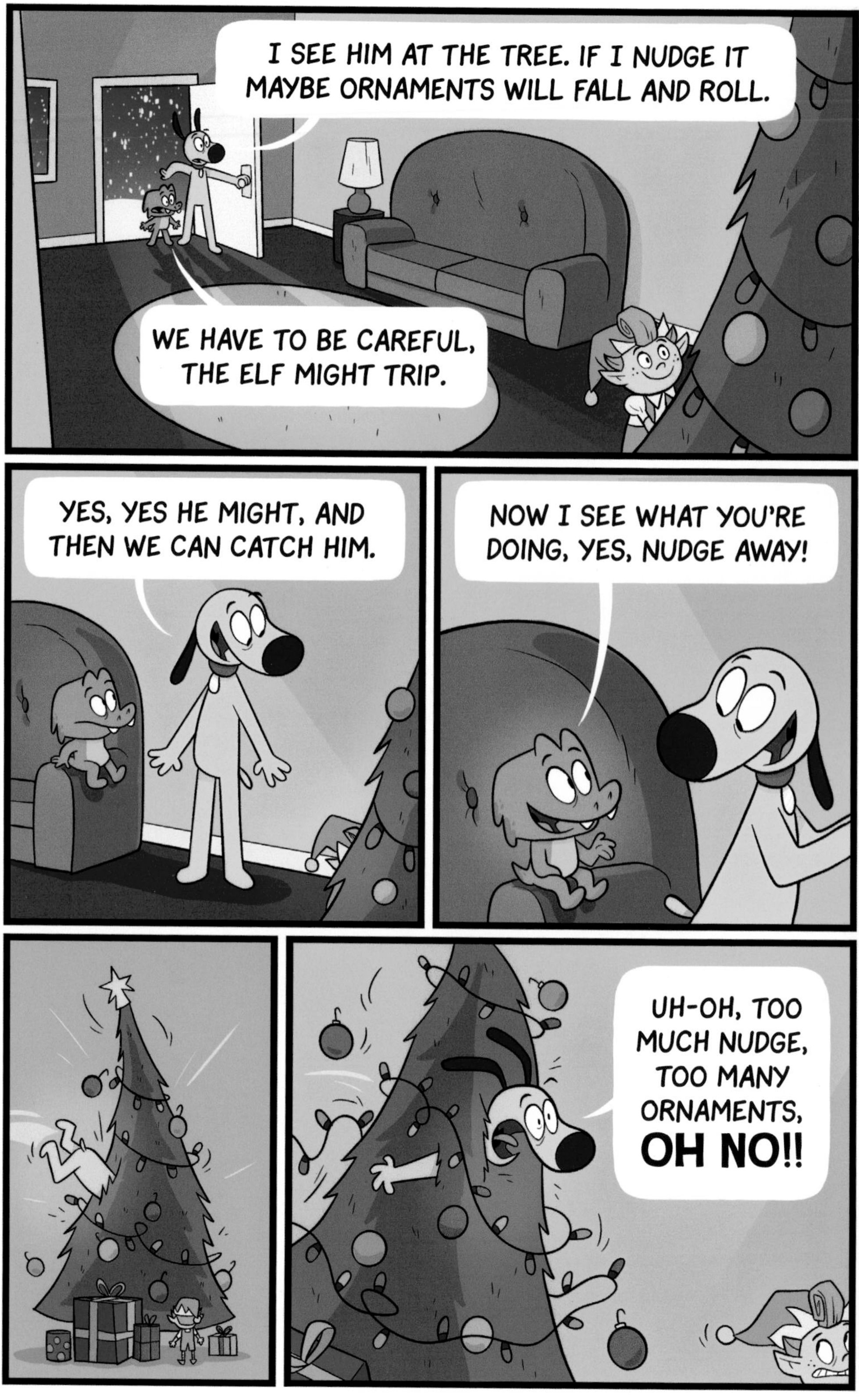
I SEE HIM AT THE TREE. IF I NUDGE IT MAYBE ORNAMENTS WILL FALL AND ROLL.
WE HAVE TO BE CAREFUL, THE ELF MIGHT TRIP.
YES, YES HE MIGHT, AND THEN WE CAN CATCH HIM.
NOW I SEE WHAT YOU'RE DOING, YES, NUDGE AWAY!
UH-OH, TOO MUCH NUDGE, TOO MANY ORNAMENTS, **OH NO!!**

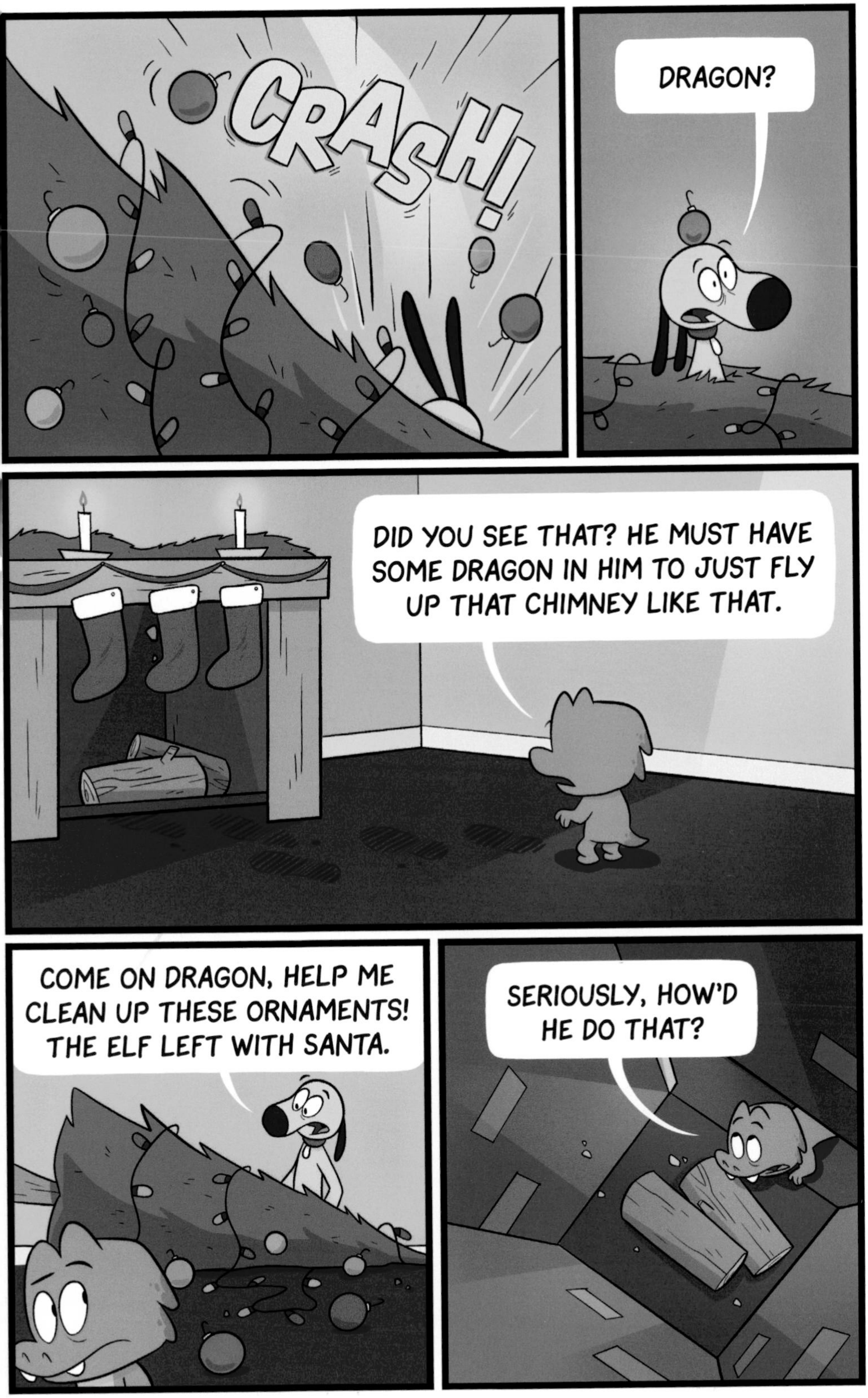
CRASH!
DRAGON?
DID YOU SEE THAT? HE MUST HAVE SOME DRAGON IN HIM TO JUST FLY UP THAT CHIMNEY LIKE THAT.
COME ON DRAGON, HELP ME CLEAN UP THESE ORNAMENTS! THE ELF LEFT WITH SANTA.
SERIOUSLY, HOW'D HE DO THAT?

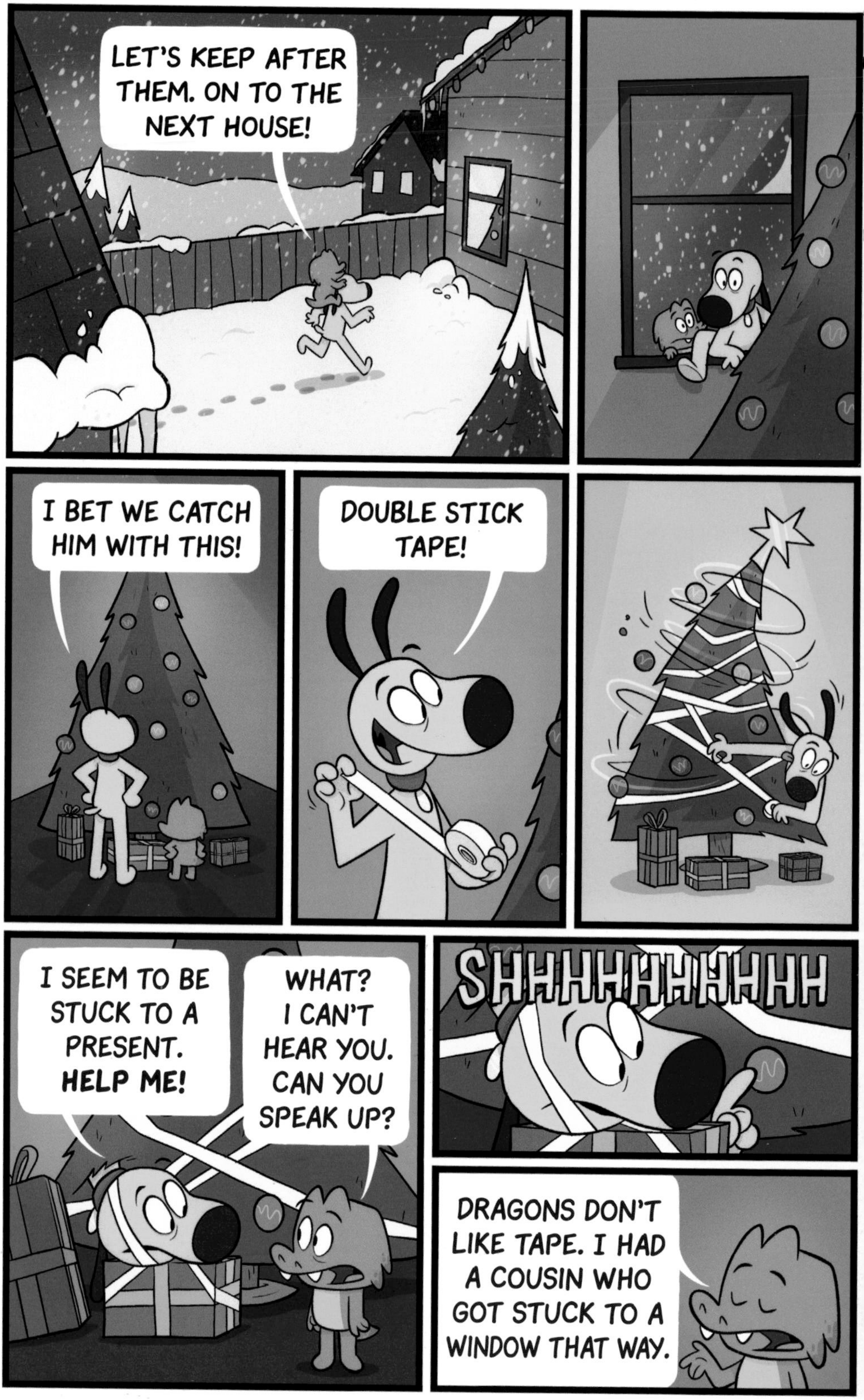
LET'S KEEP AFTER THEM. ON TO THE NEXT HOUSE!
I BET WE CATCH HIM WITH THIS!
DOUBLE STICK TAPE!
I SEEM TO BE STUCK TO A PRESENT. **HELP ME!**
WHAT? I CAN'T HEAR YOU. CAN YOU SPEAK UP?
SHHHHHHHHHH
DRAGONS DON'T LIKE TAPE. I HAD A COUSIN WHO GOT STUCK TO A WINDOW THAT WAY.

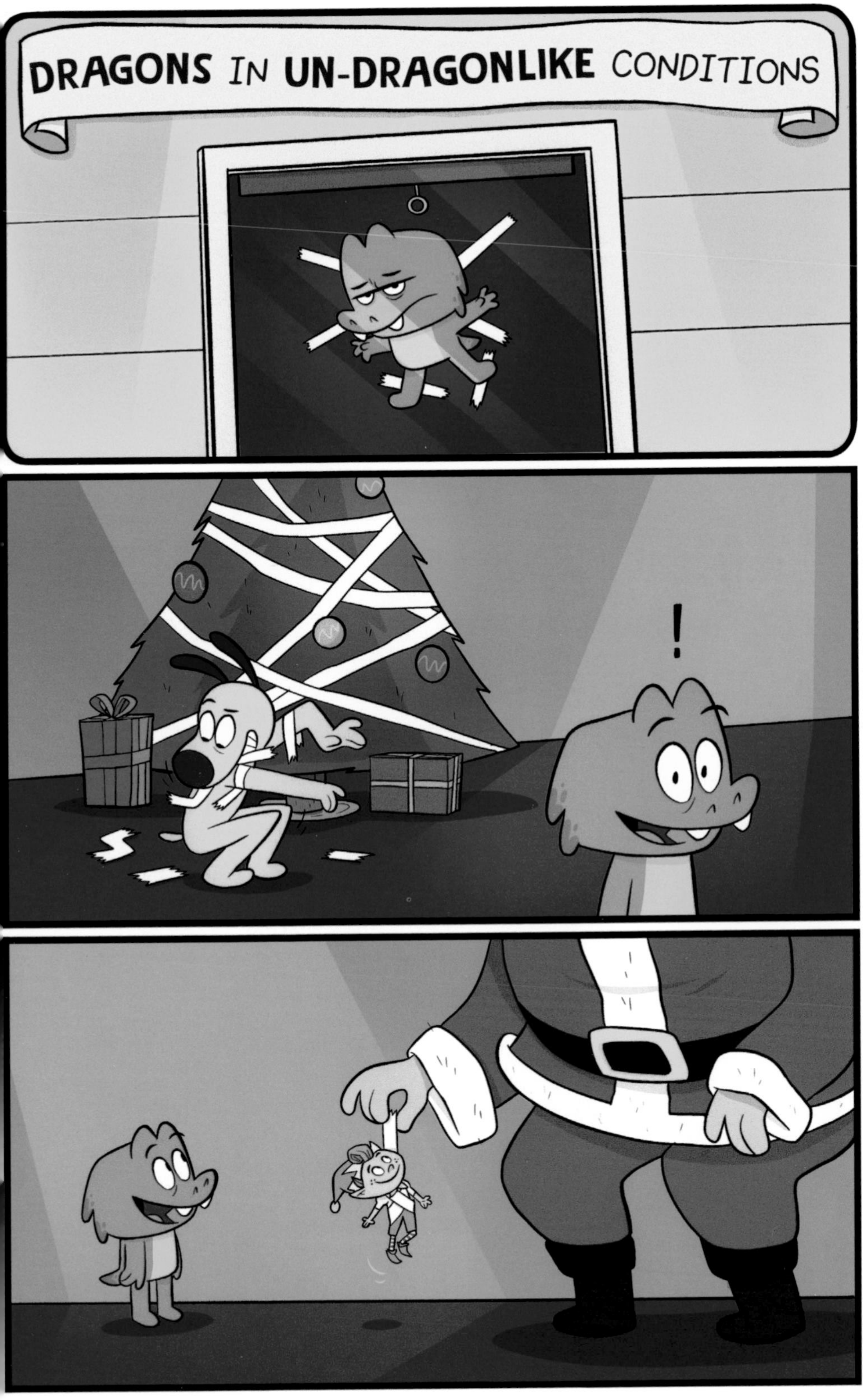
DRAGONS IN UN-DRAGONLIKE CONDITIONS
!

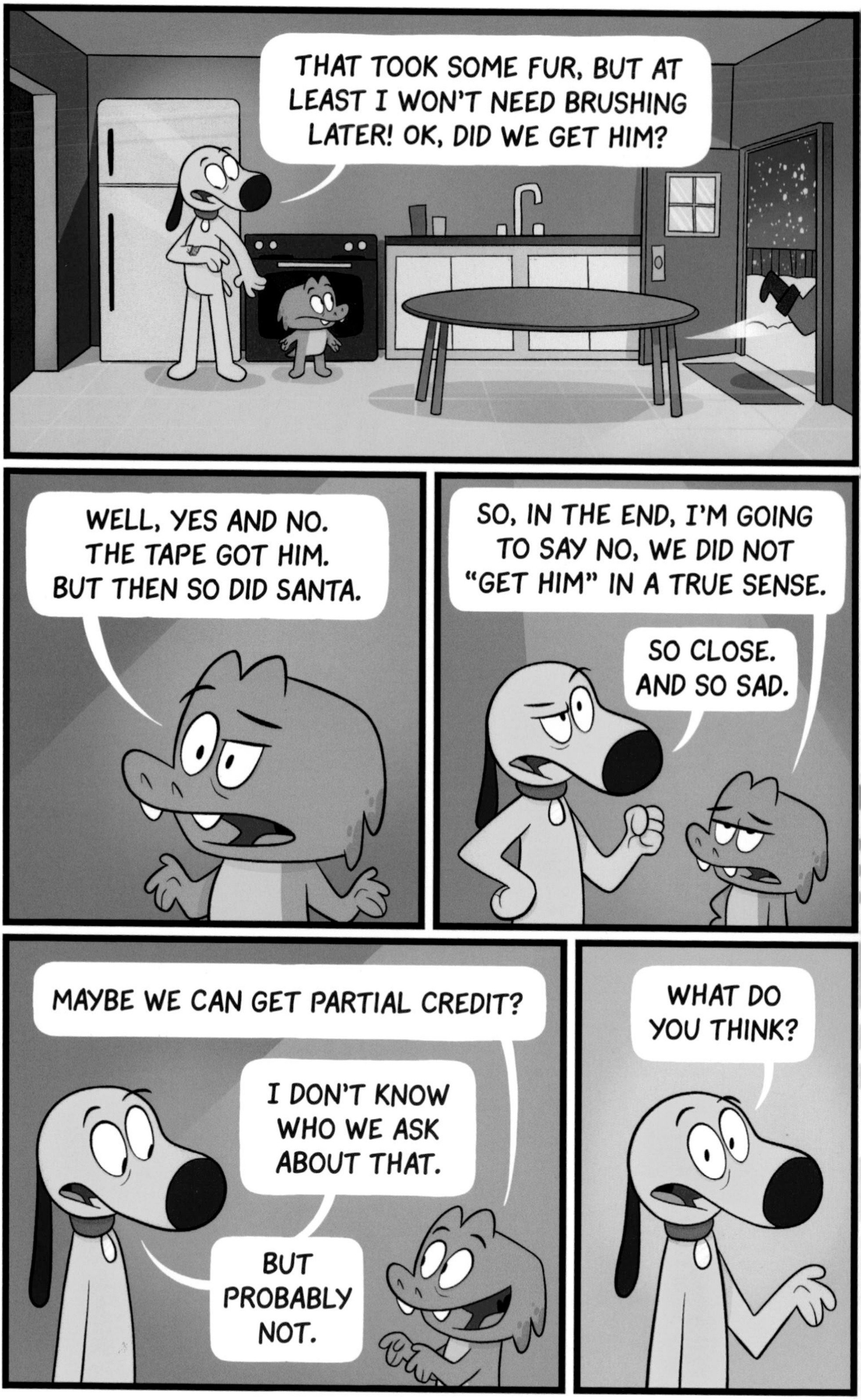
THAT TOOK SOME FUR, BUT AT LEAST I WON'T NEED BRUSHING LATER! OK, DID WE GET HIM?
WELL, YES AND NO. THE TAPE GOT HIM. BUT THEN SO DID SANTA.
SO, IN THE END, I'M GOING TO SAY NO, WE DID NOT "GET HIM" IN A TRUE SENSE.
SO CLOSE. AND SO SAD.
MAYBE WE CAN GET PARTIAL CREDIT?
I DON'T KNOW WHO WE ASK ABOUT THAT.
BUT PROBABLY NOT.
WHAT DO YOU THINK?

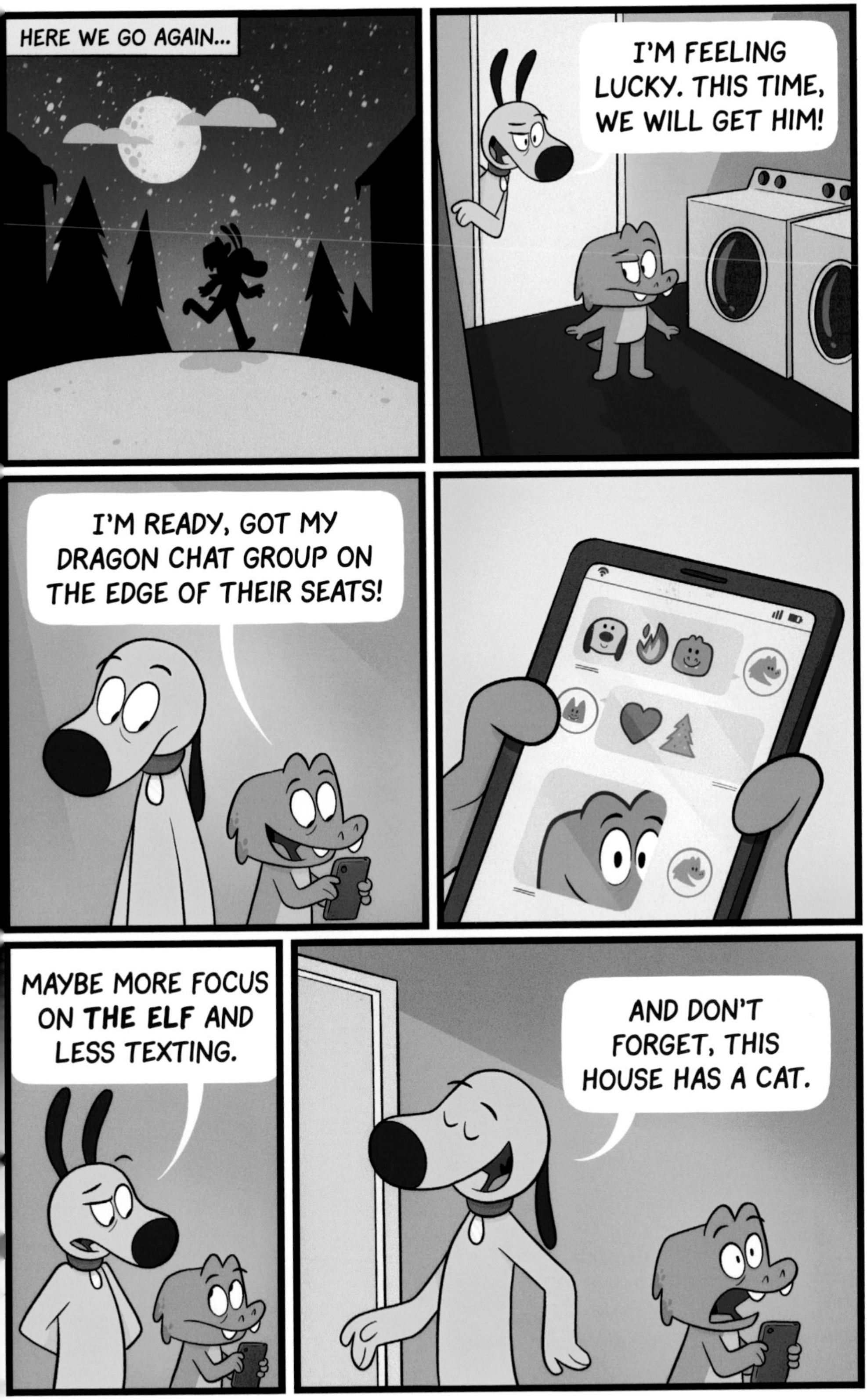
HERE WE GO AGAIN...
I'M FEELING LUCKY. THIS TIME, WE WILL GET HIM!
I'M READY, GOT MY DRAGON CHAT GROUP ON THE EDGE OF THEIR SEATS!
MAYBE MORE FOCUS ON **THE ELF** AND LESS TEXTING.
AND DON'T FORGET, THIS HOUSE HAS A CAT.

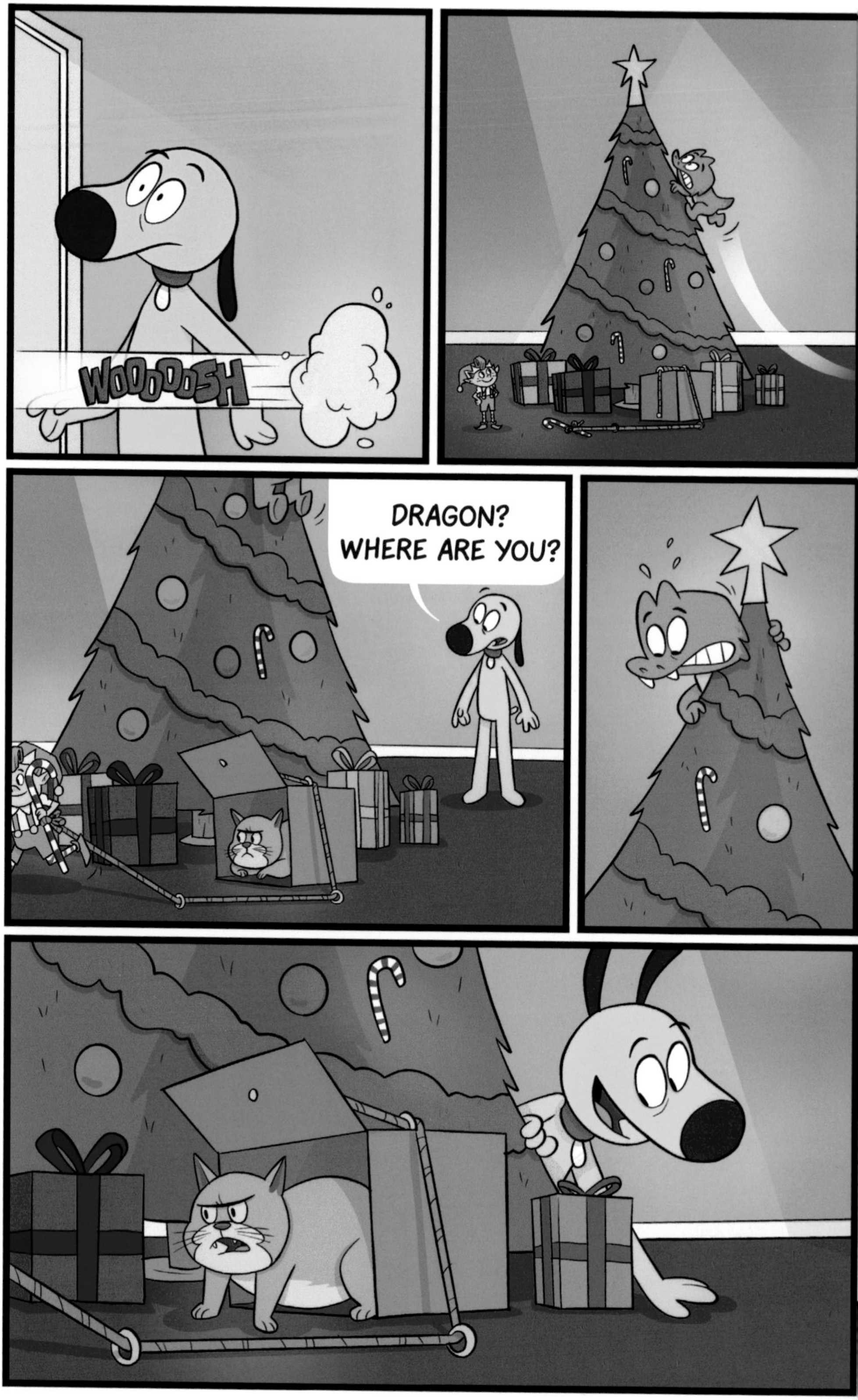
WOOOOOSH
DRAGON? WHERE ARE YOU?

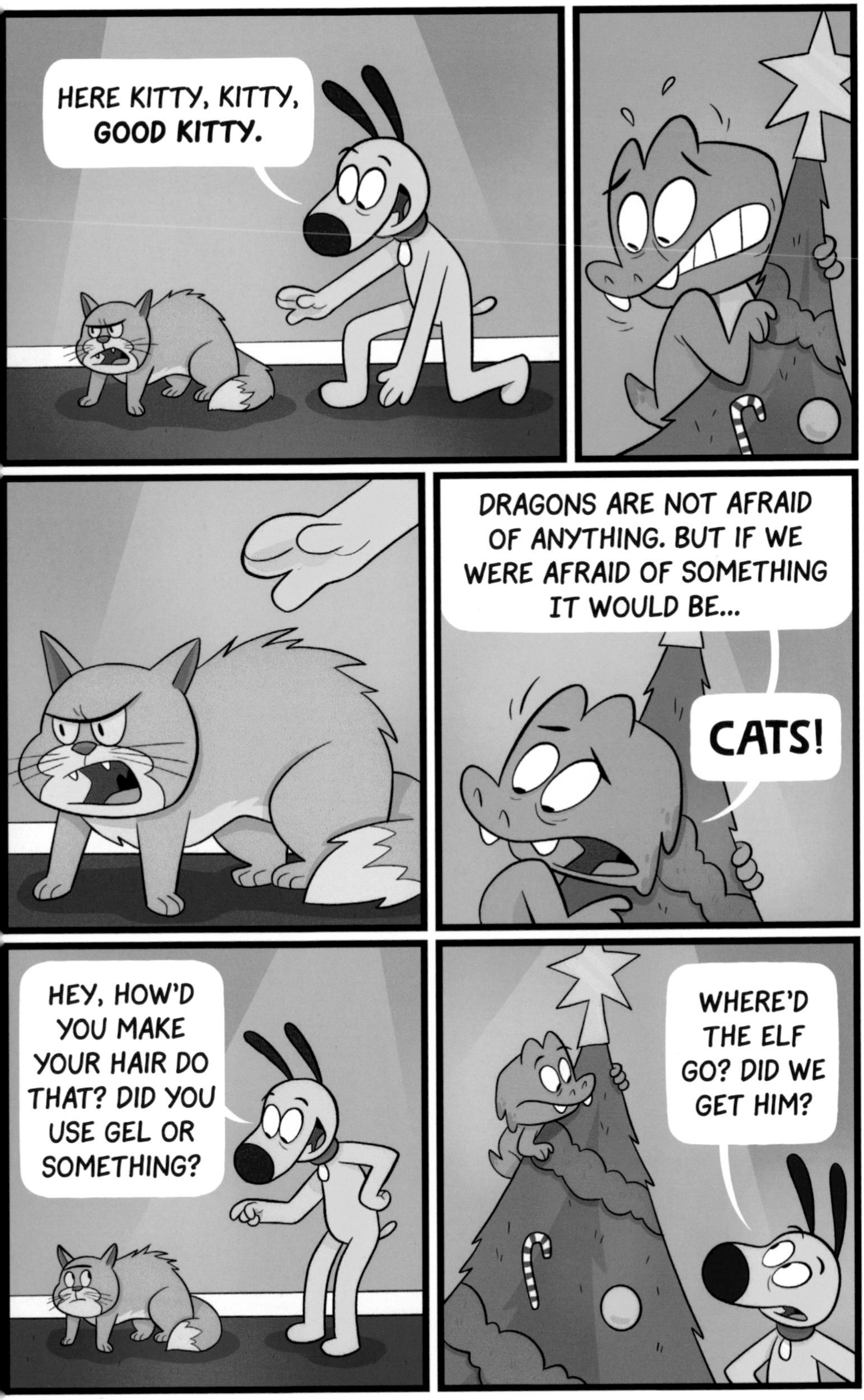
HERE KITTY, KITTY, GOOD KITTY.
DRAGONS ARE NOT AFRAID OF ANYTHING. BUT IF WE WERE AFRAID OF SOMETHING IT WOULD BE...
CATS!
HEY, HOW'D YOU MAKE YOUR HAIR DO THAT? DID YOU USE GEL OR SOMETHING?
WHERE'D THE ELF GO? DID WE GET HIM?

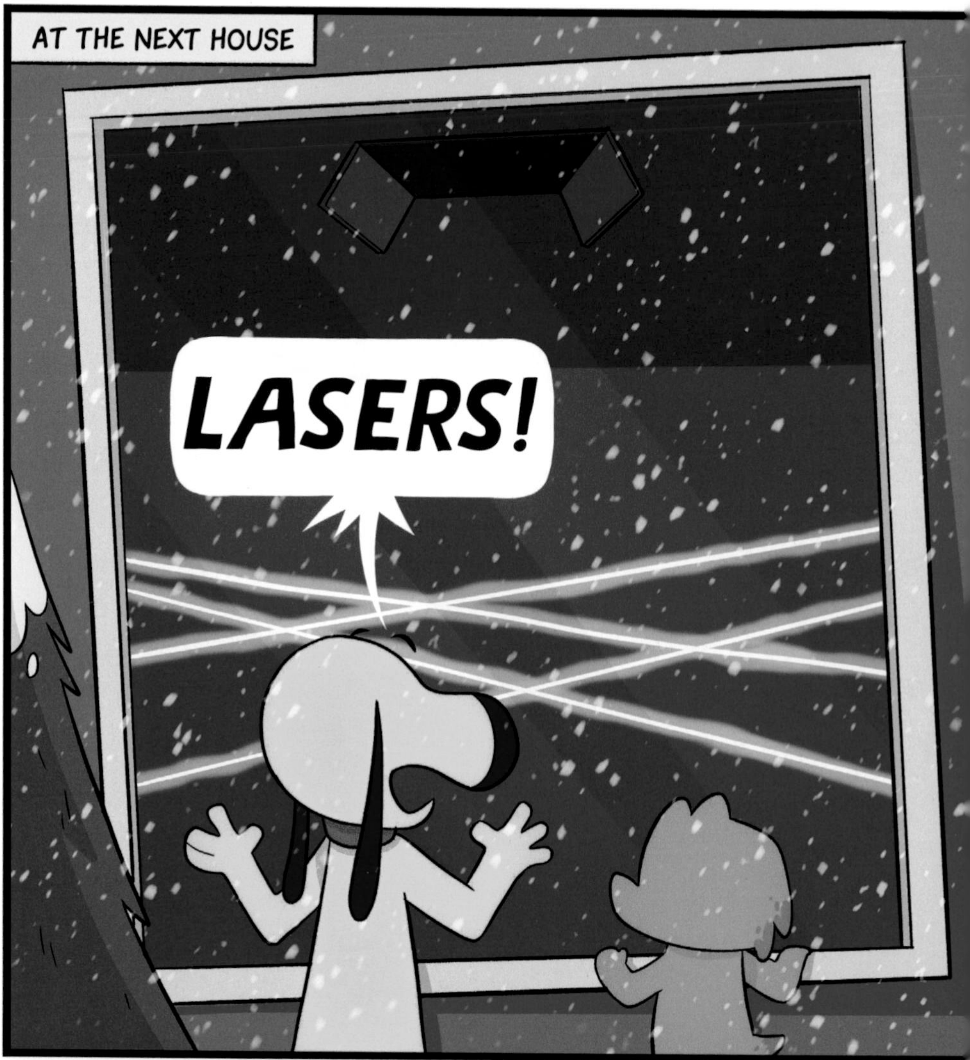
AT THE NEXT HOUSE
LASERS!

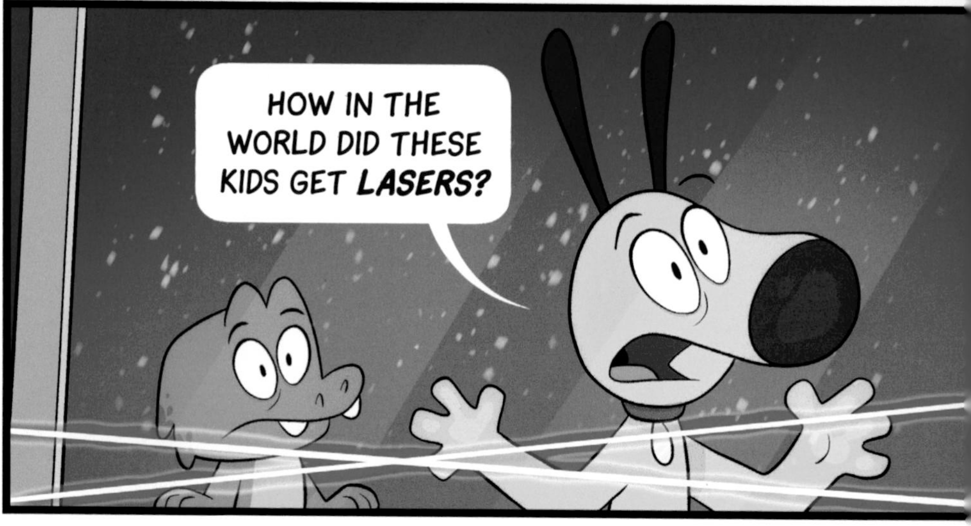
HOW IN THE WORLD DID THESE KIDS GET LASERS?

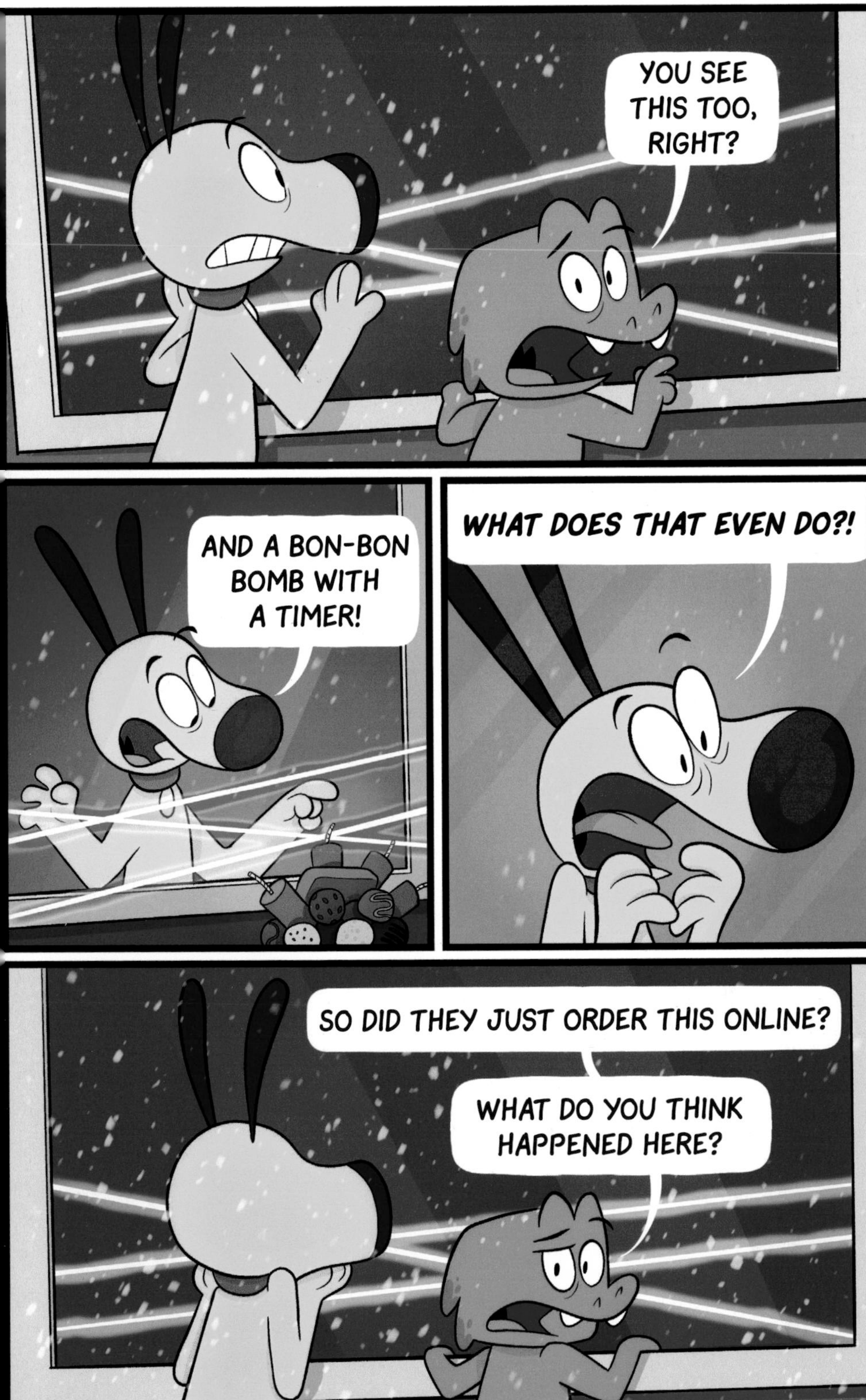

YOU SEE THIS TOO, RIGHT?
AND A BON-BON BOMB WITH A TIMER!
WHAT DOES THAT EVEN DO?!
SO DID THEY JUST ORDER THIS ONLINE?
WHAT DO YOU THINK HAPPENED HERE?

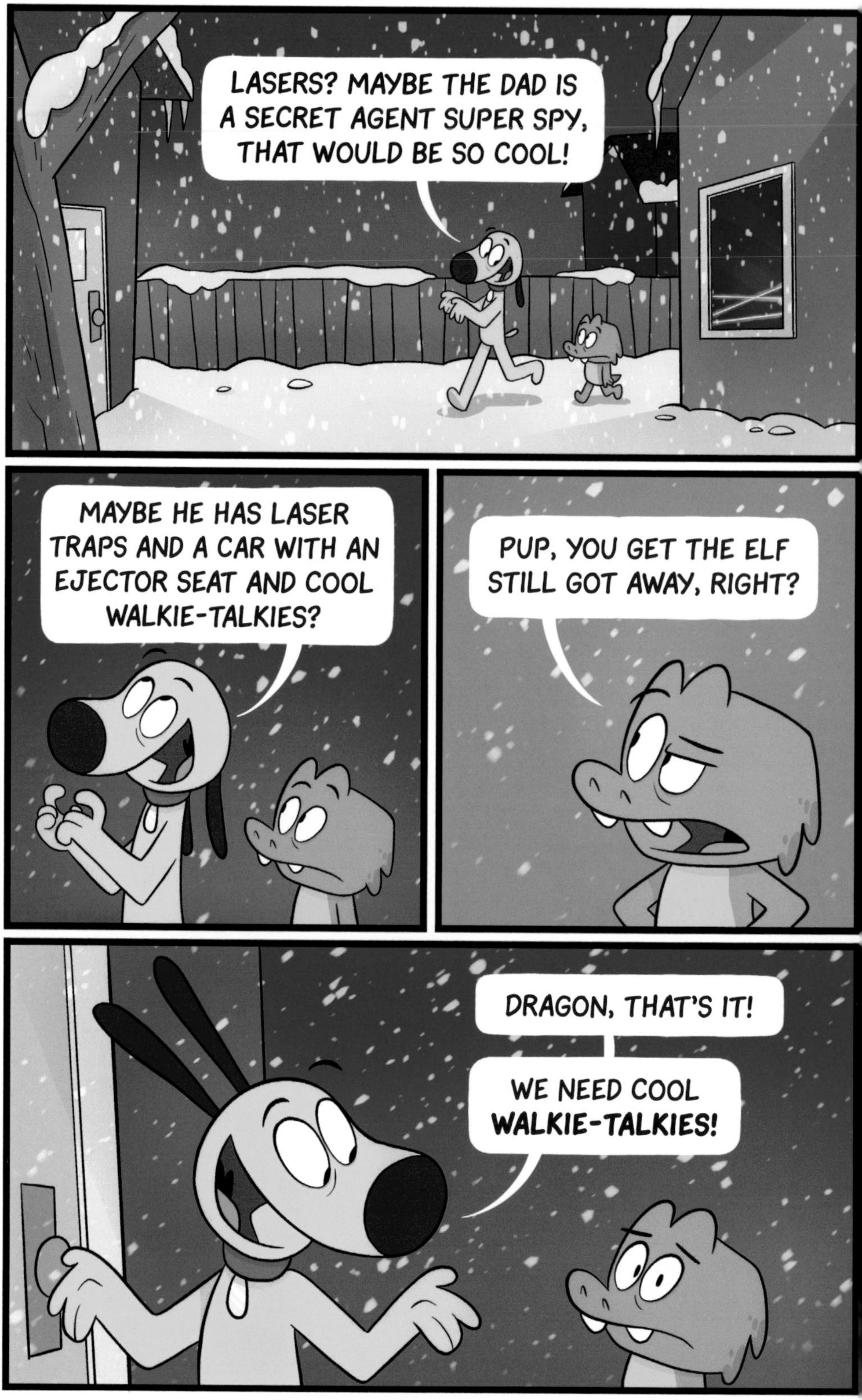
LASERS? MAYBE THE DAD IS A SECRET AGENT SUPER SPY, THAT WOULD BE SO COOL!
MAYBE HE HAS LASER TRAPS AND A CAR WITH AN EJECTOR SEAT AND COOL WALKIE-TALKIES?
PUP, YOU GET THE ELF STILL GOT AWAY, RIGHT?
DRAGON, THAT'S IT!
WE NEED COOL WALKIE-TALKIES!

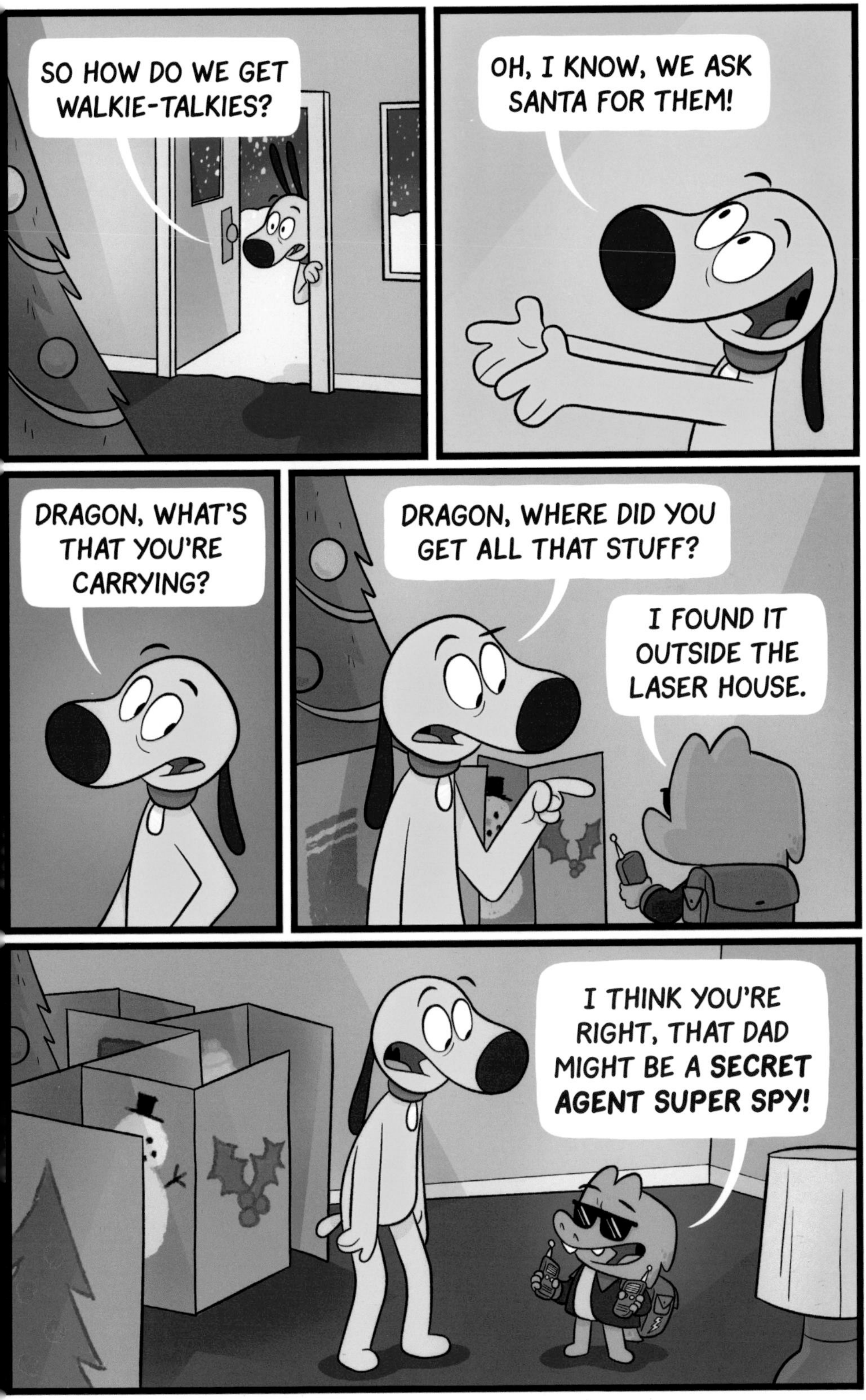
SO HOW DO WE GET WALKIE-TALKIES?
OH, I KNOW, WE ASK SANTA FOR THEM!
DRAGON, WHAT'S THAT YOU'RE CARRYING?
DRAGON, WHERE DID YOU GET ALL THAT STUFF?
I FOUND IT OUTSIDE THE LASER HOUSE.
I THINK YOU'RE RIGHT, THAT DAD MIGHT BE A **SECRET AGENT SUPER SPY!**

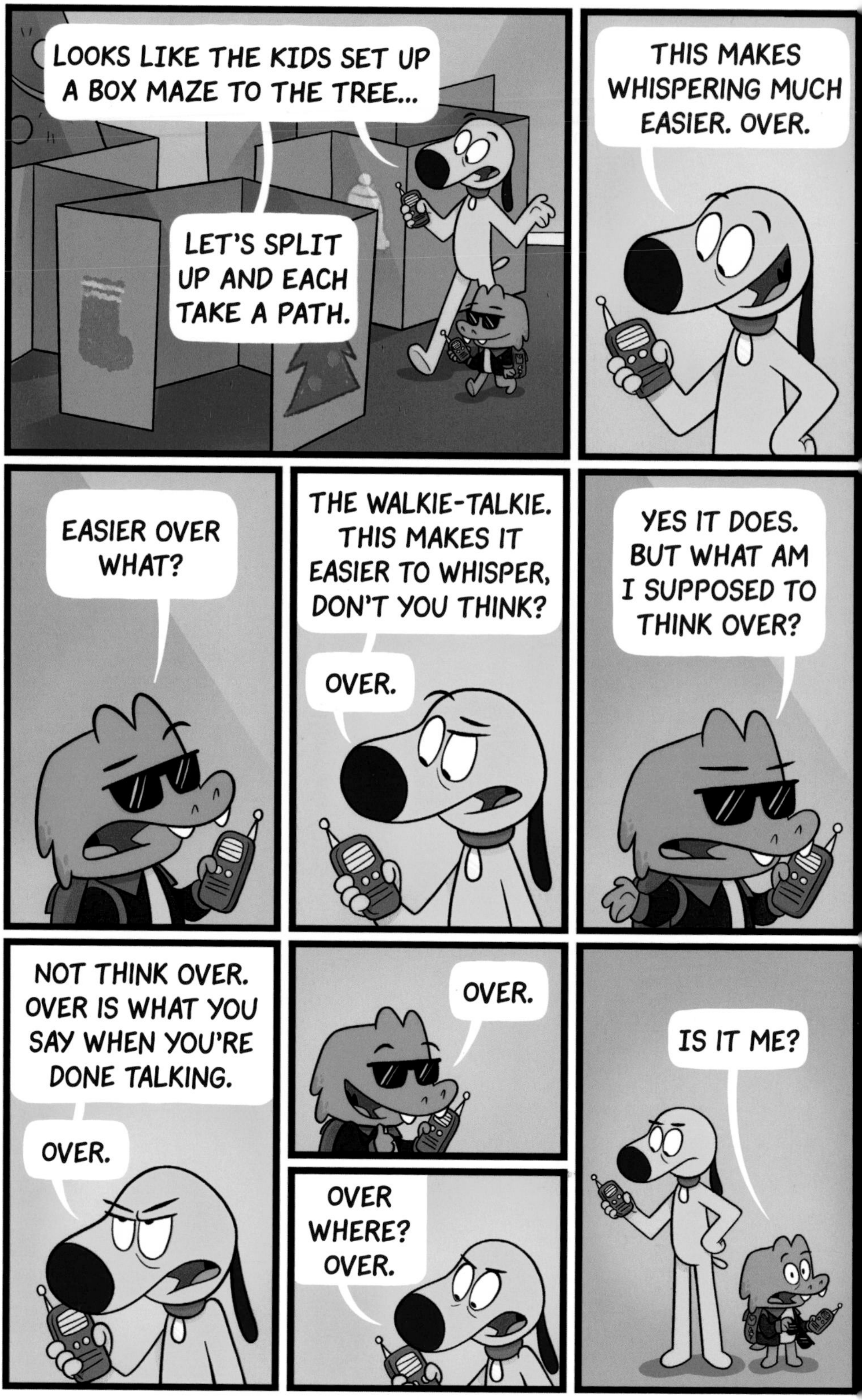
LOOKS LIKE THE KIDS SET UP A BOX MAZE TO THE TREE...
LET'S SPLIT UP AND EACH TAKE A PATH.
THIS MAKES WHISPERING MUCH EASIER. OVER.
EASIER OVER WHAT?
THE WALKIE-TALKIE. THIS MAKES IT EASIER TO WHISPER, DON'T YOU THINK?
OVER.
YES IT DOES. BUT WHAT AM I SUPPOSED TO THINK OVER?
NOT THINK OVER. OVER IS WHAT YOU SAY WHEN YOU'RE DONE TALKING.
OVER.
OVER.
OVER WHERE? OVER.
IS IT ME?

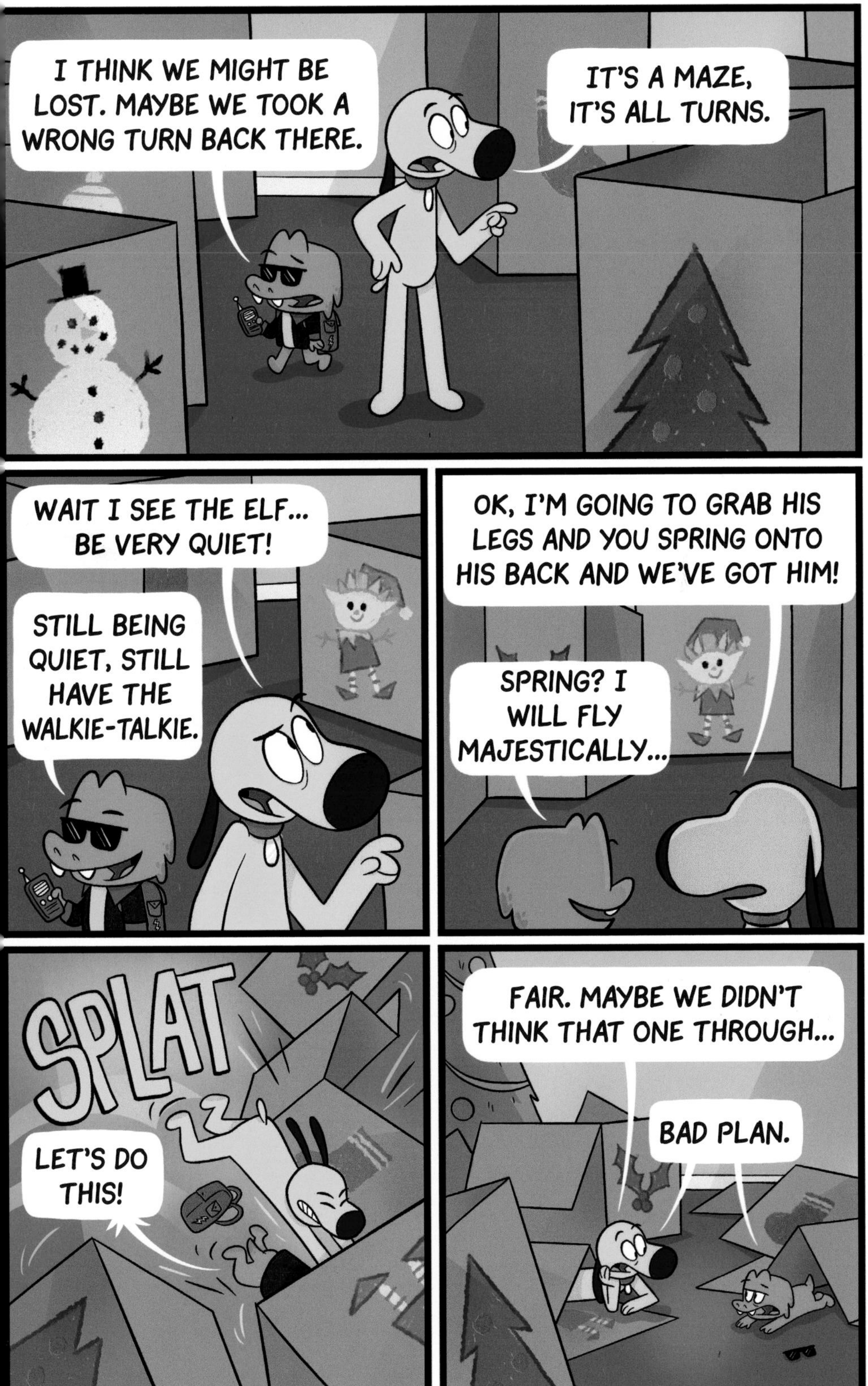
I THINK WE MIGHT BE LOST. MAYBE WE TOOK A WRONG TURN BACK THERE.
IT'S A MAZE, IT'S ALL TURNS.
WAIT I SEE THE ELF... BE VERY QUIET!
STILL BEING QUIET, STILL HAVE THE WALKIE-TALKIE.
OK, I'M GOING TO GRAB HIS LEGS AND YOU SPRING ONTO HIS BACK AND WE'VE GOT HIM!
SPRING? I WILL FLY MAJESTICALLY...
SPLAT
LET'S DO THIS!
FAIR. MAYBE WE DIDN'T THINK THAT ONE THROUGH...
BAD PLAN.

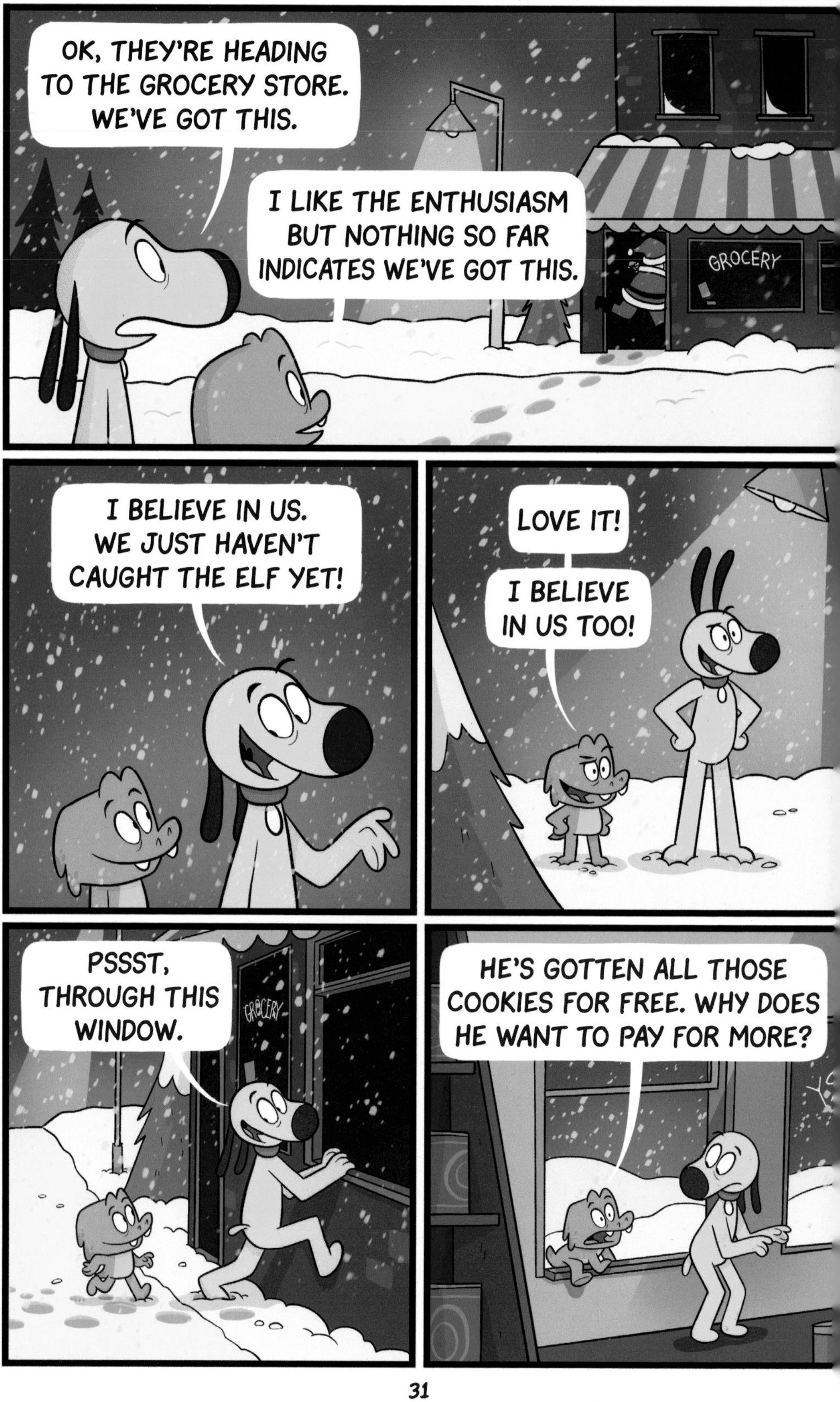
OK, THEY'RE HEADING TO THE GROCERY STORE. WE'VE GOT THIS.
I LIKE THE ENTHUSIASM BUT NOTHING SO FAR INDICATES WE'VE GOT THIS.
GROCERY
I BELIEVE IN US. WE JUST HAVEN'T CAUGHT THE ELF YET!
LOVE IT!
I BELIEVE IN US TOO!
PSSST, THROUGH THIS WINDOW.
GROCERY
HE'S GOTTEN ALL THOSE COOKIES FOR FREE. WHY DOES HE WANT TO PAY FOR MORE?

PUP, ANY IDEA WHY A GROCERY STORE WOULD HAVE A CANNON?

I MEAN, THAT'S WEIRD RIGHT?

I DON'T SEE THEM, DO YOU?

I'M MORE CONCERNED THAT I SEE A CANNON.

I BET HE'S LOOKING FOR MILK, THAT WOULD MAKE SENSE. SO MANY COOKIES.

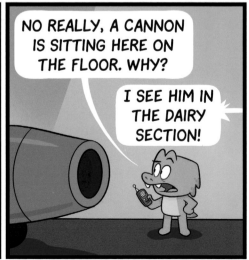

NO REALLY, A CANNON IS SITTING HERE ON THE FLOOR. WHY?

I SEE HIM IN THE DAIRY SECTION!

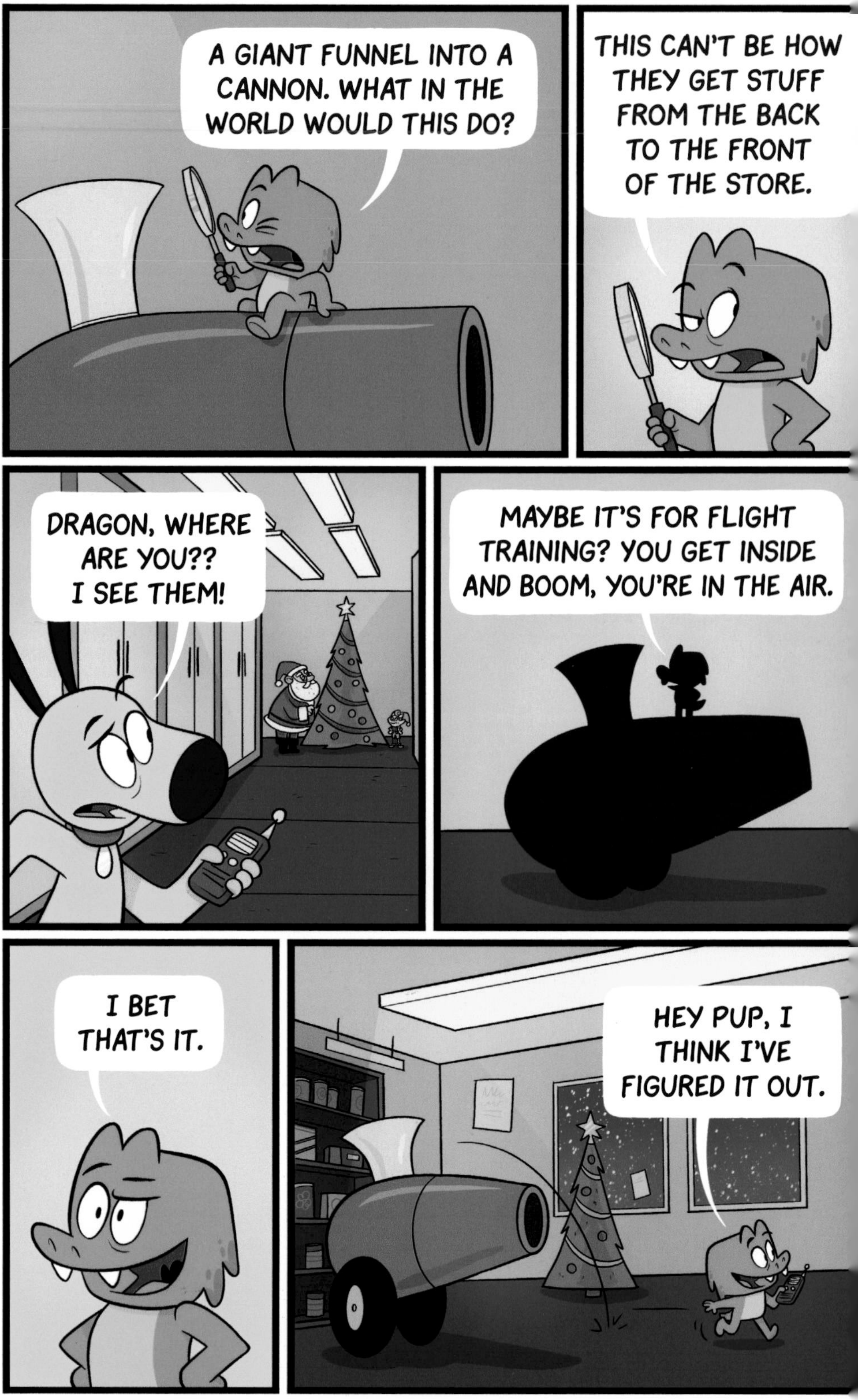
A GIANT FUNNEL INTO A CANNON. WHAT IN THE WORLD WOULD THIS DO?
THIS CAN'T BE HOW THEY GET STUFF FROM THE BACK TO THE FRONT OF THE STORE.
DRAGON, WHERE ARE YOU?? I SEE THEM!
MAYBE IT'S FOR FLIGHT TRAINING? YOU GET INSIDE AND BOOM, YOU'RE IN THE AIR.
I BET THAT'S IT.
HEY PUP, I THINK I'VE FIGURED IT OUT.

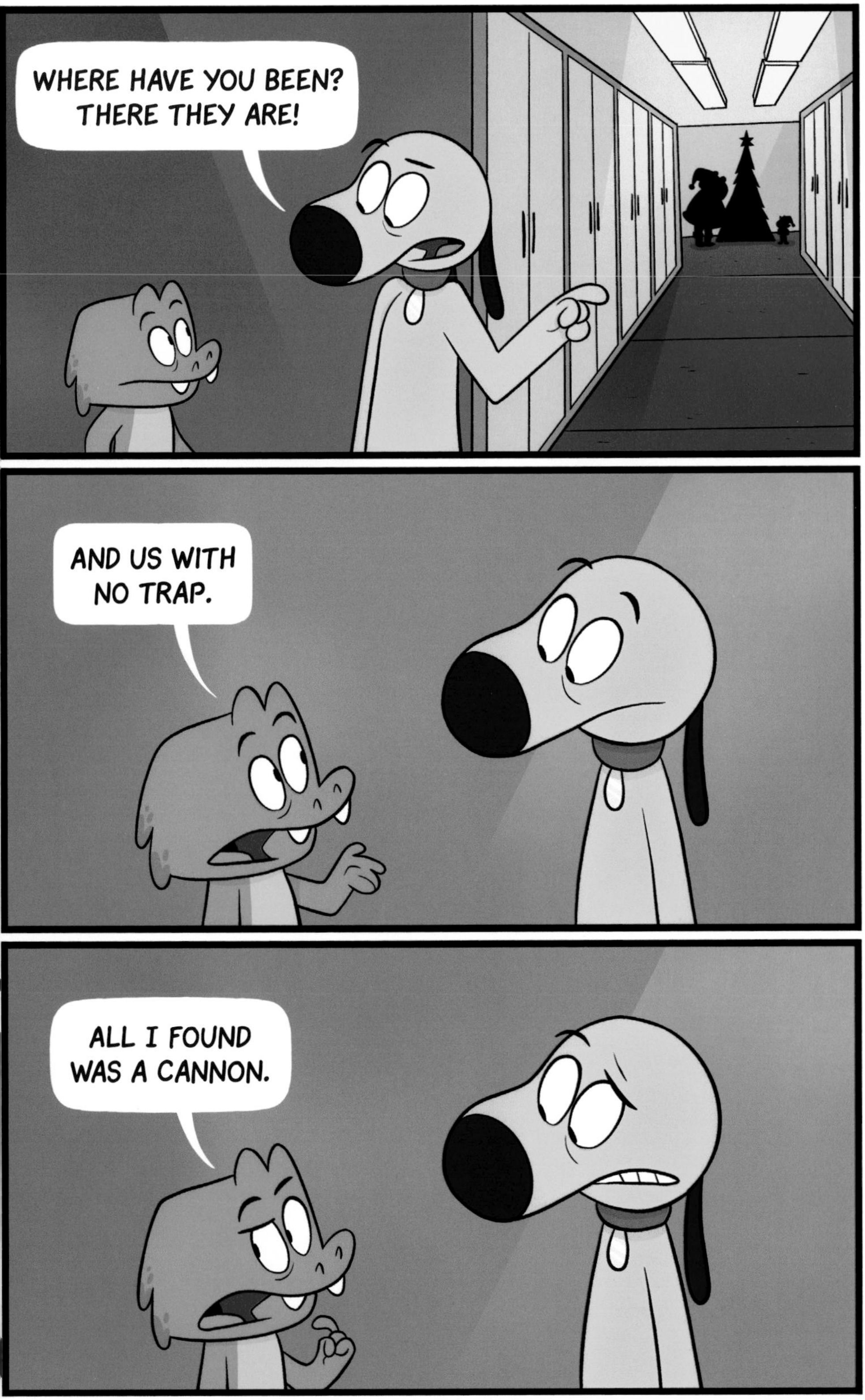
WHERE HAVE YOU BEEN? THERE THEY ARE!
AND US WITH NO TRAP.
ALL I FOUND WAS A CANNON.

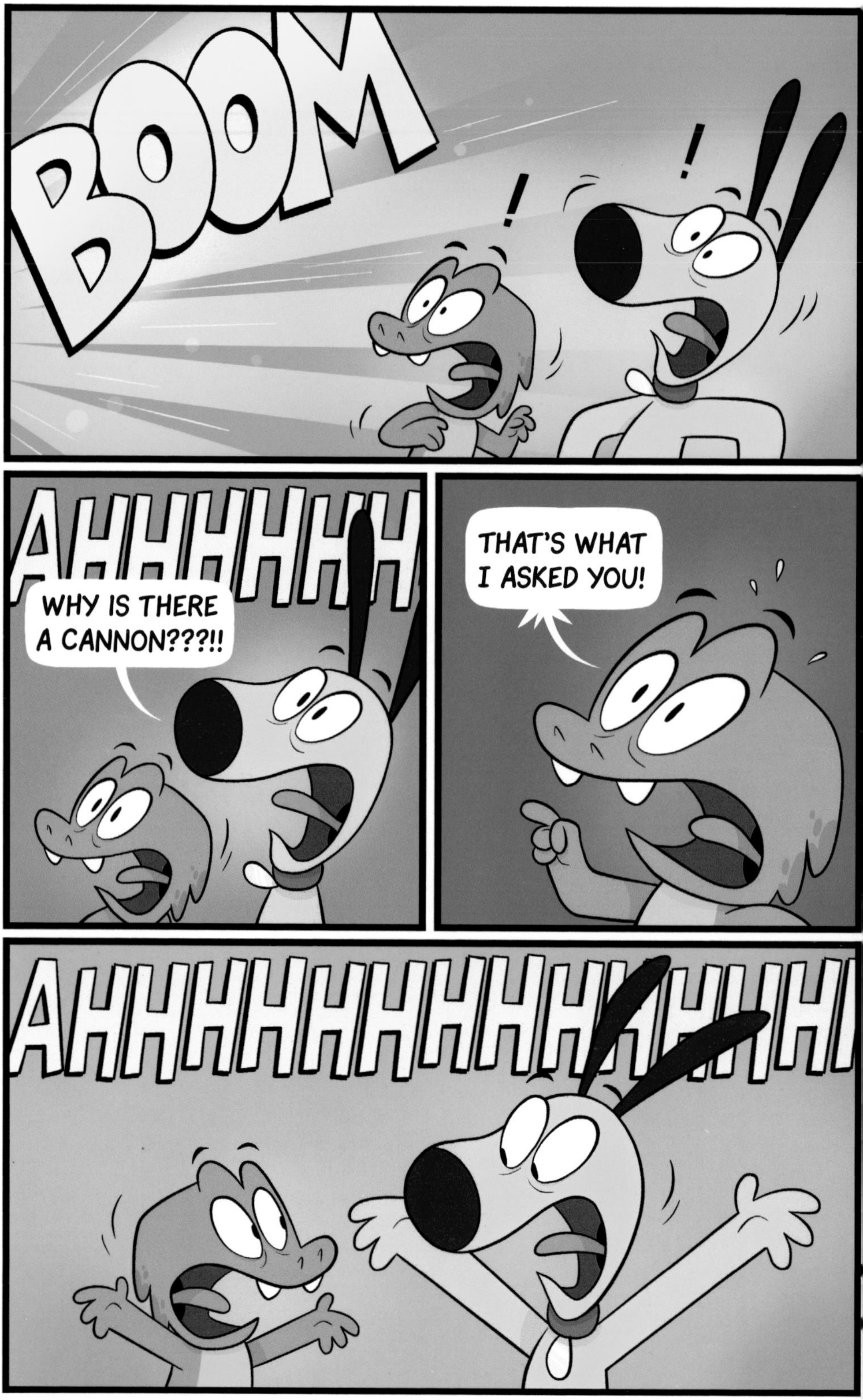
BOOM
!
!
AHHHHHH
WHY IS THERE A CANNON???!!
THAT'S WHAT I ASKED YOU!
AHHHHHHHHHHHHHHH

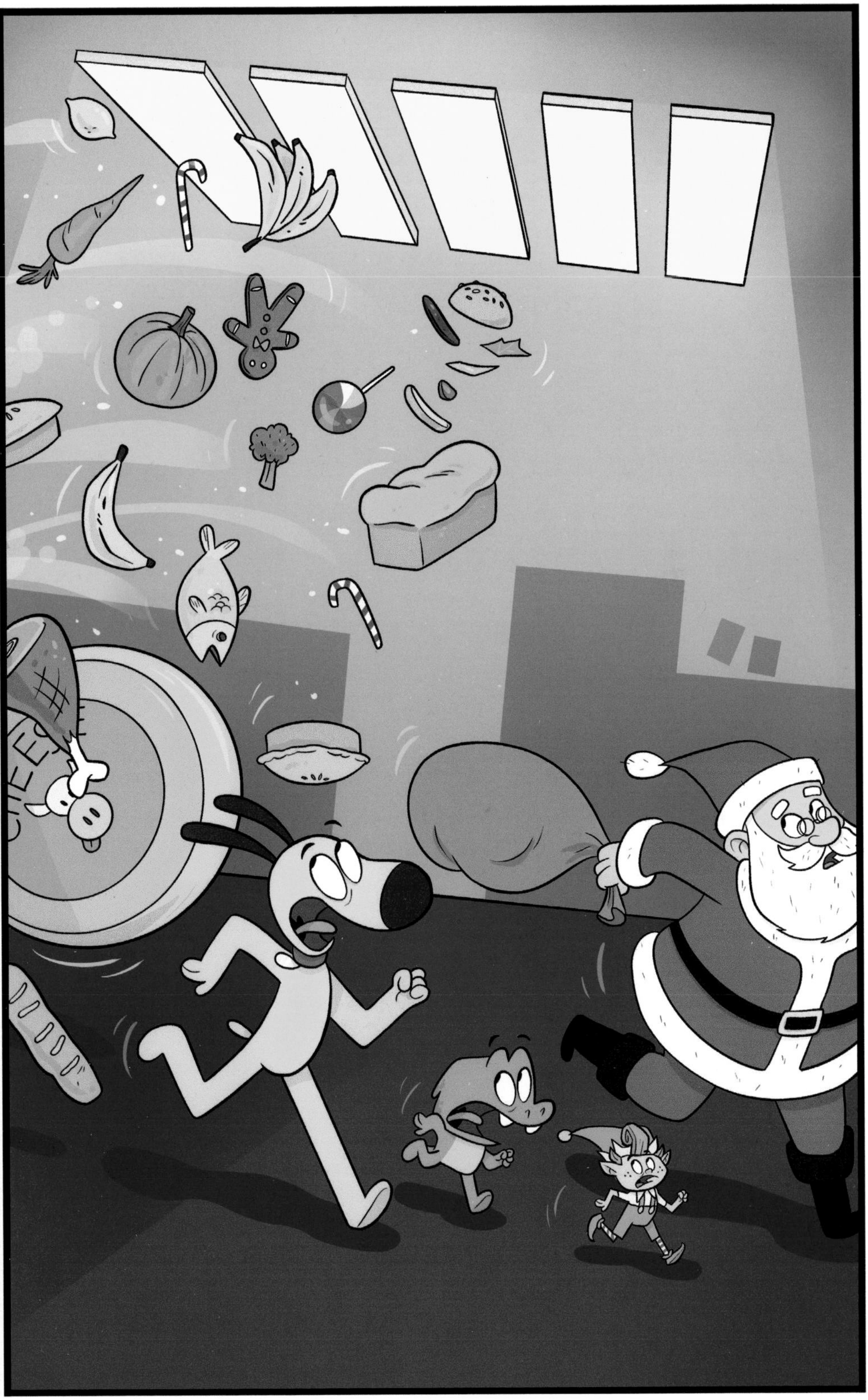

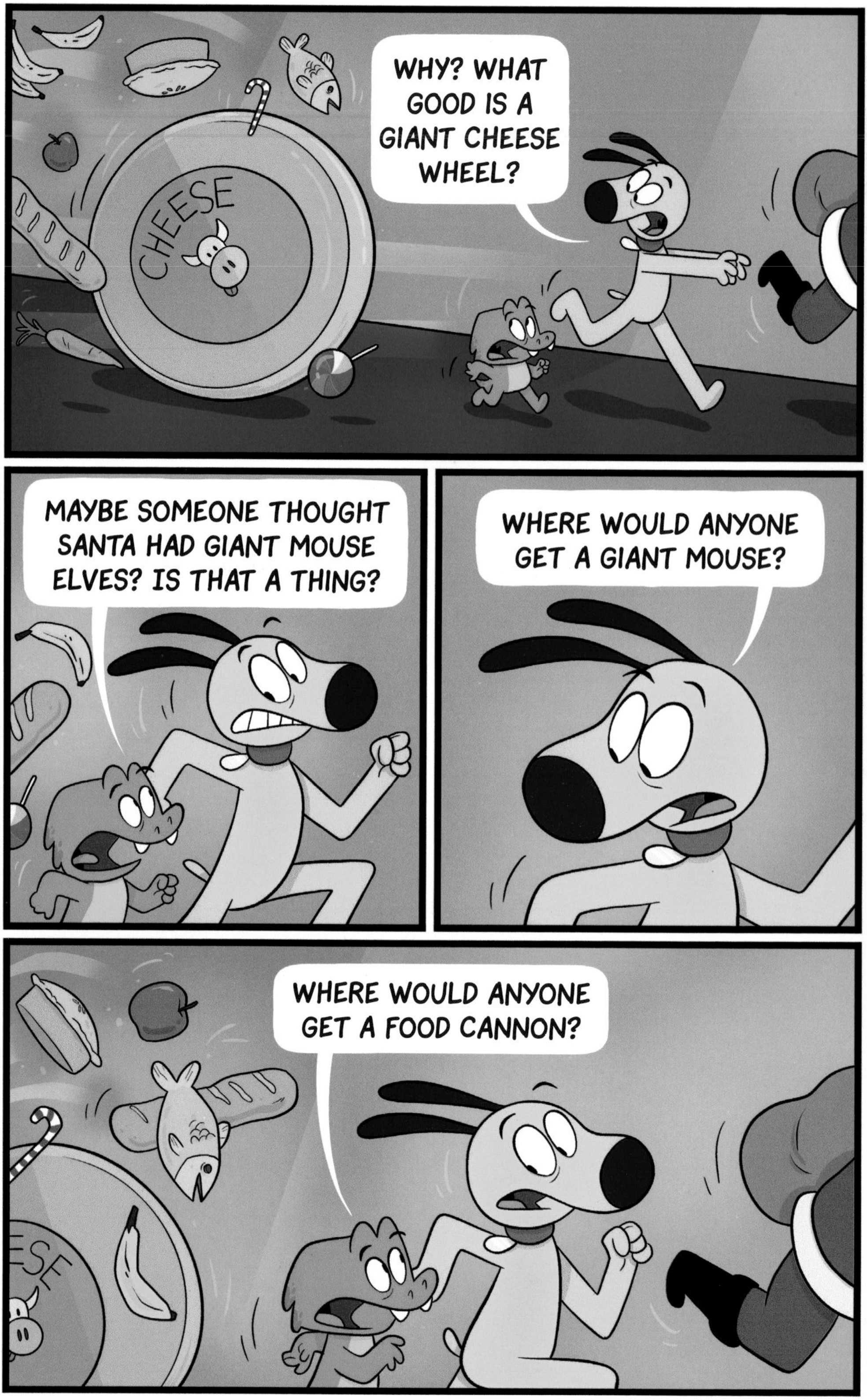
CHEESE
WHY? WHAT GOOD IS A GIANT CHEESE WHEEL?
MAYBE SOMEONE THOUGHT SANTA HAD GIANT MOUSE ELVES? IS THAT A THING?
WHERE WOULD ANYONE GET A GIANT MOUSE?
WHERE WOULD ANYONE GET A FOOD CANNON?

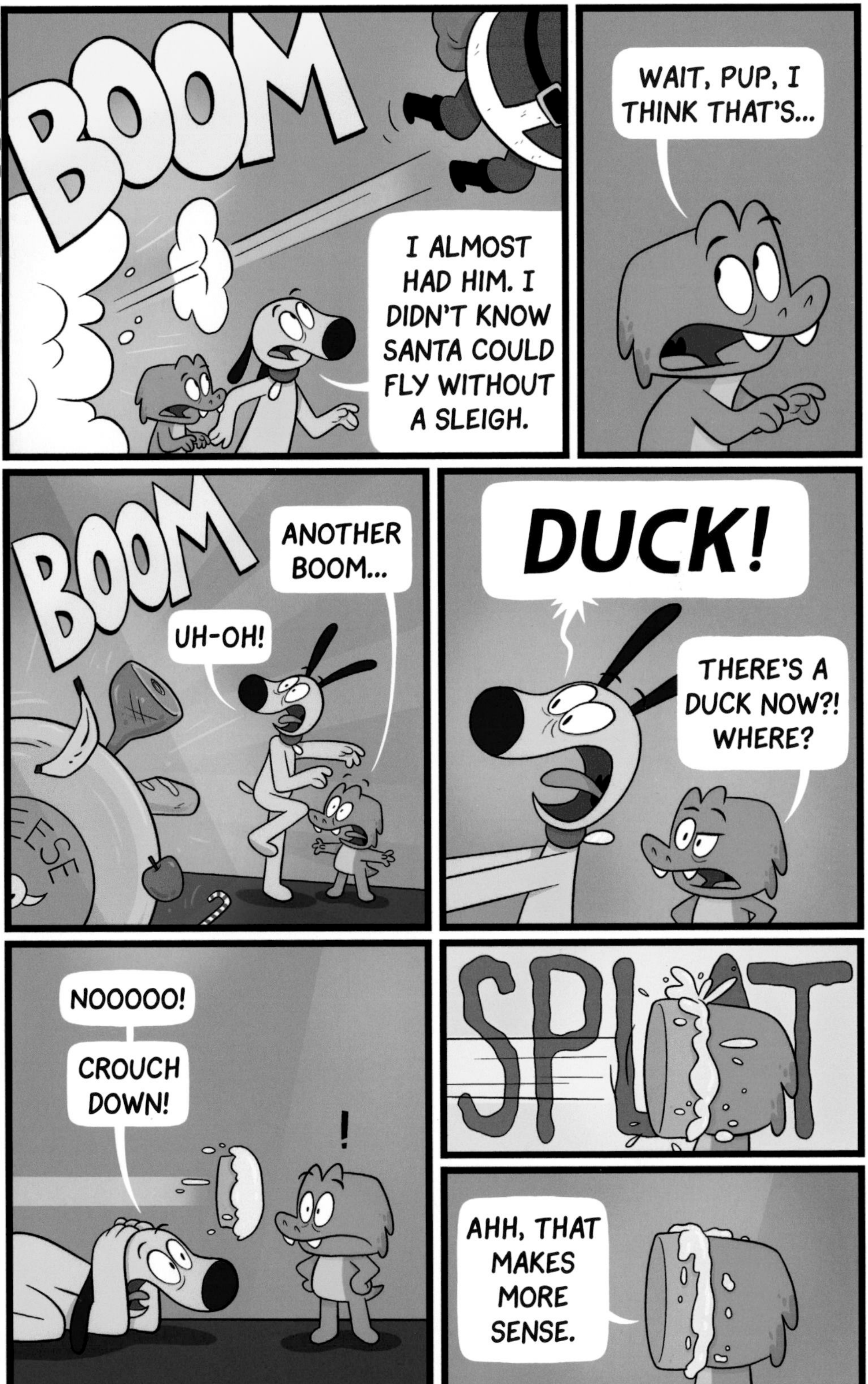
BOOM
I ALMOST HAD HIM. I DIDN'T KNOW SANTA COULD FLY WITHOUT A SLEIGH.
WAIT, PUP, I THINK THAT'S...
BOOM
ANOTHER BOOM...
UH-OH!
DUCK!
THERE'S A DUCK NOW?! WHERE?
NOOOOO!
CROUCH DOWN!
!
SPLAT
AHH, THAT MAKES MORE SENSE.

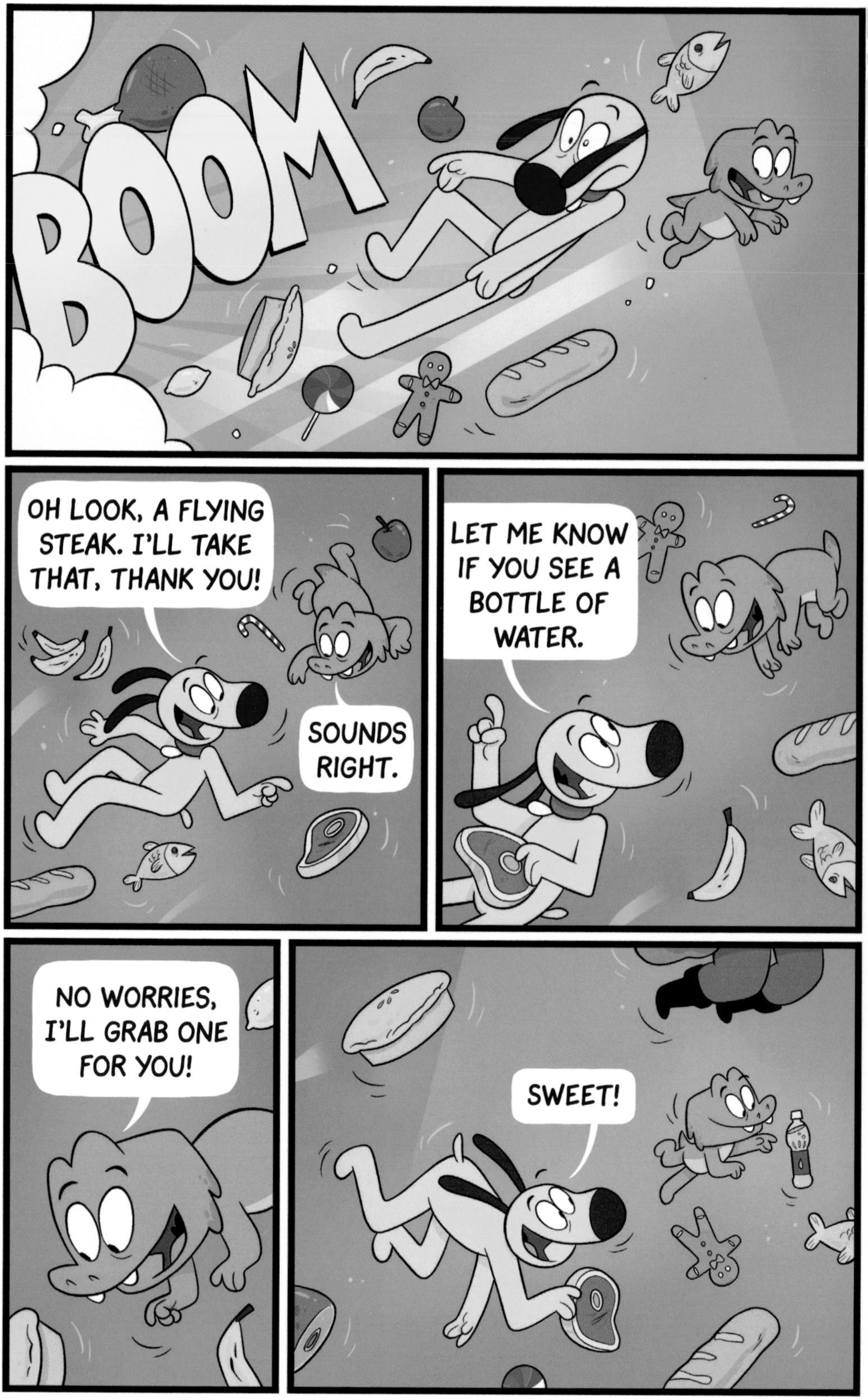
BOOM
OH LOOK, A FLYING STEAK. I'LL TAKE THAT, THANK YOU!
SOUNDS RIGHT.
LET ME KNOW IF YOU SEE A BOTTLE OF WATER.
NO WORRIES, I'LL GRAB ONE FOR YOU!
SWEET!

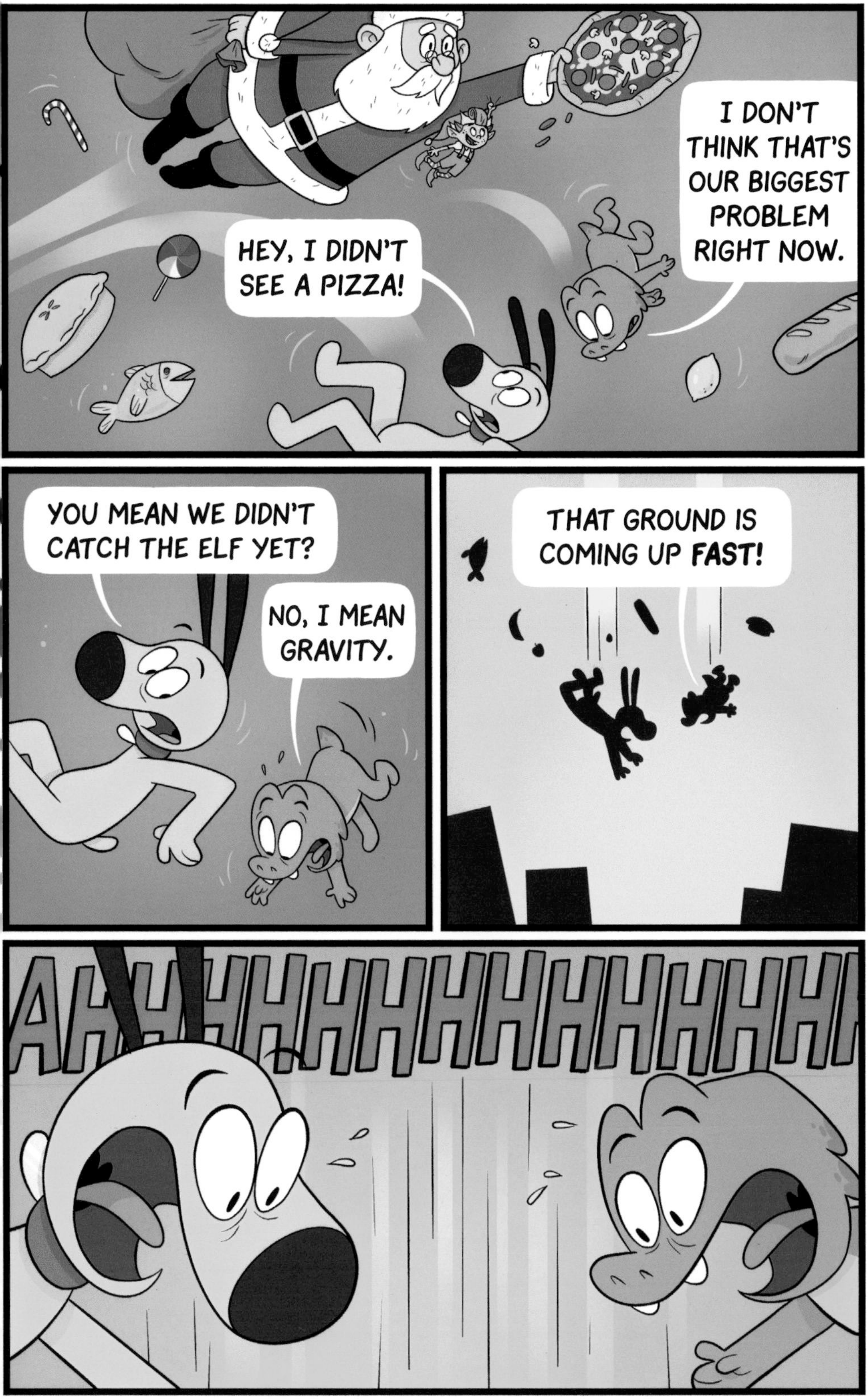
HEY, I DIDN'T SEE A PIZZA!
I DON'T THINK THAT'S OUR BIGGEST PROBLEM RIGHT NOW.
YOU MEAN WE DIDN'T CATCH THE ELF YET?
NO, I MEAN GRAVITY.
THAT GROUND IS COMING UP **FAST**!
AHHHHHHHHHHHHHHHHHH

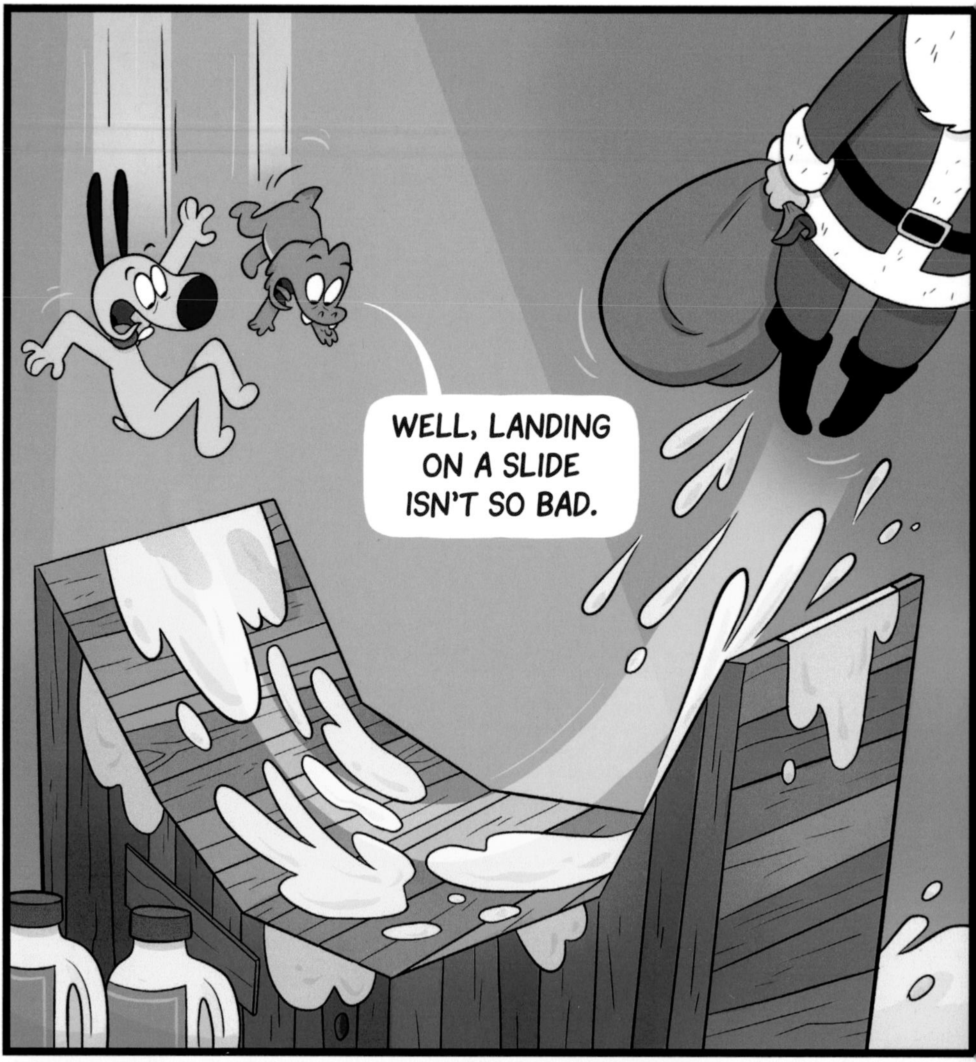
WELL, LANDING ON A SLIDE ISN'T SO BAD.

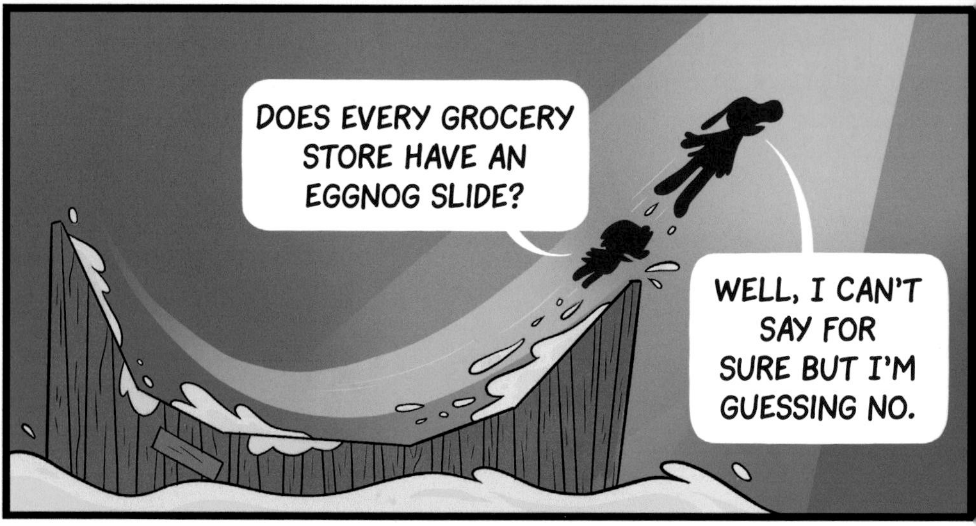
DOES EVERY GROCERY STORE HAVE AN EGGNOG SLIDE?
WELL, I CAN'T SAY FOR SURE BUT I'M GUESSING NO.

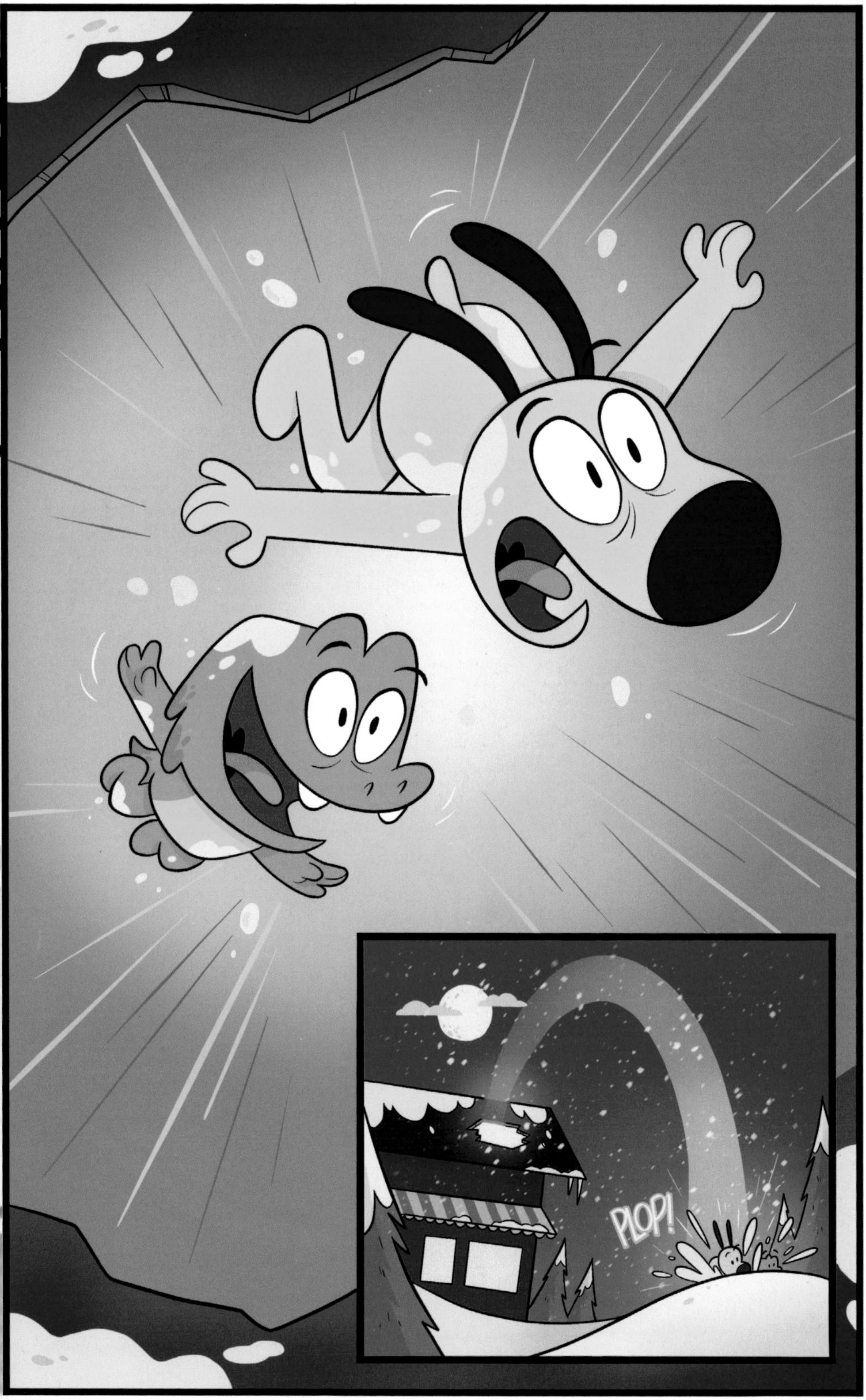
PLOP!

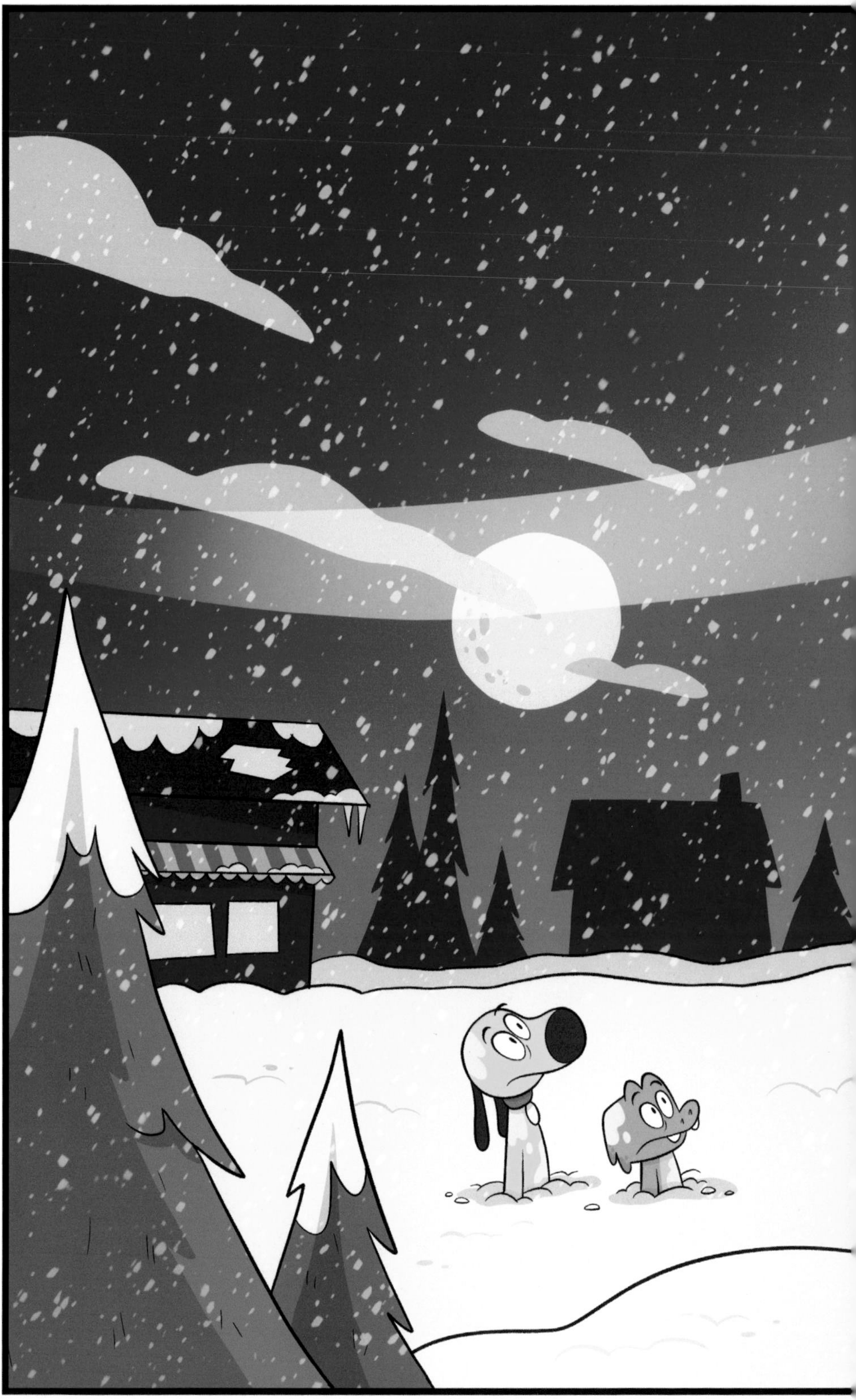

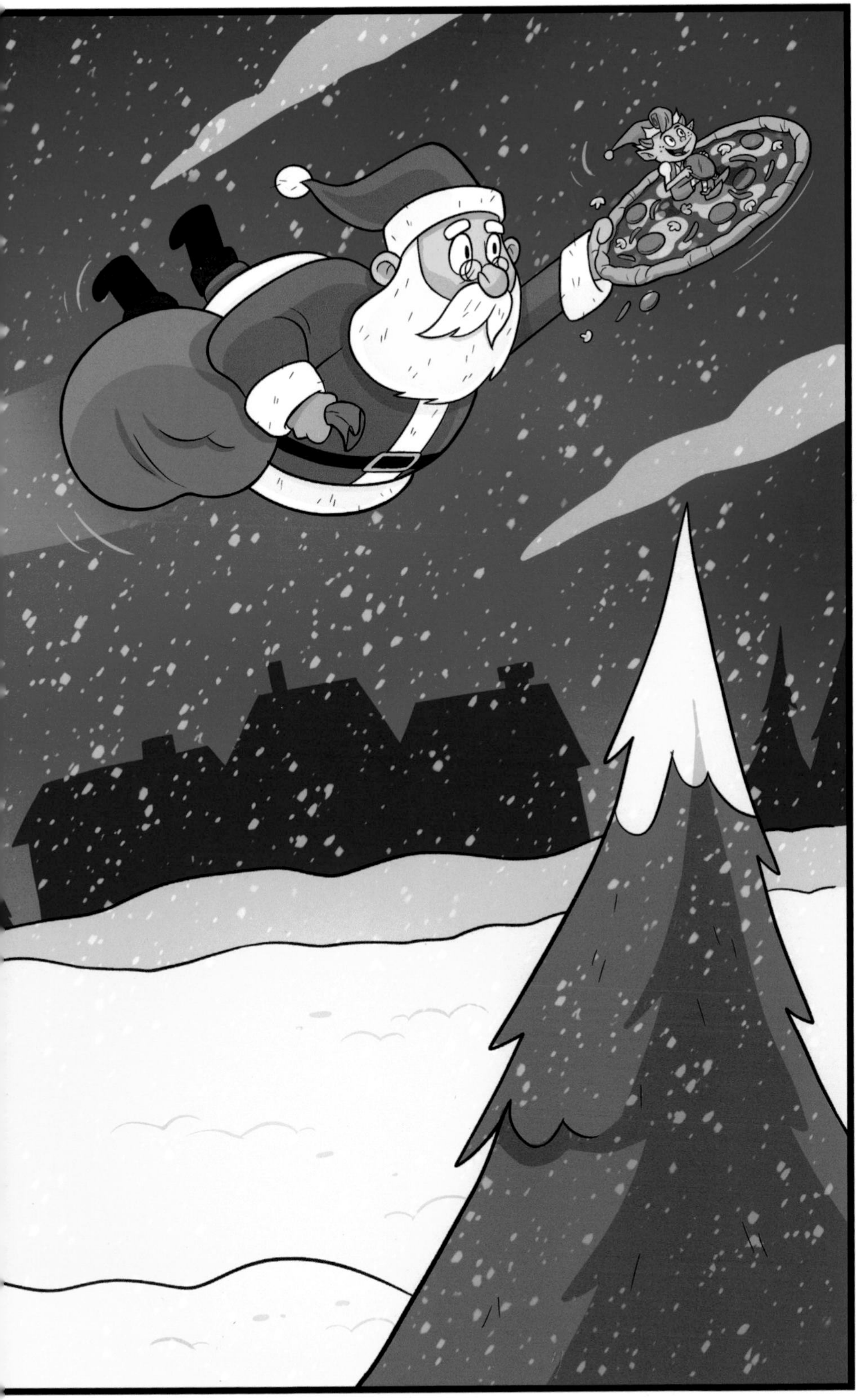

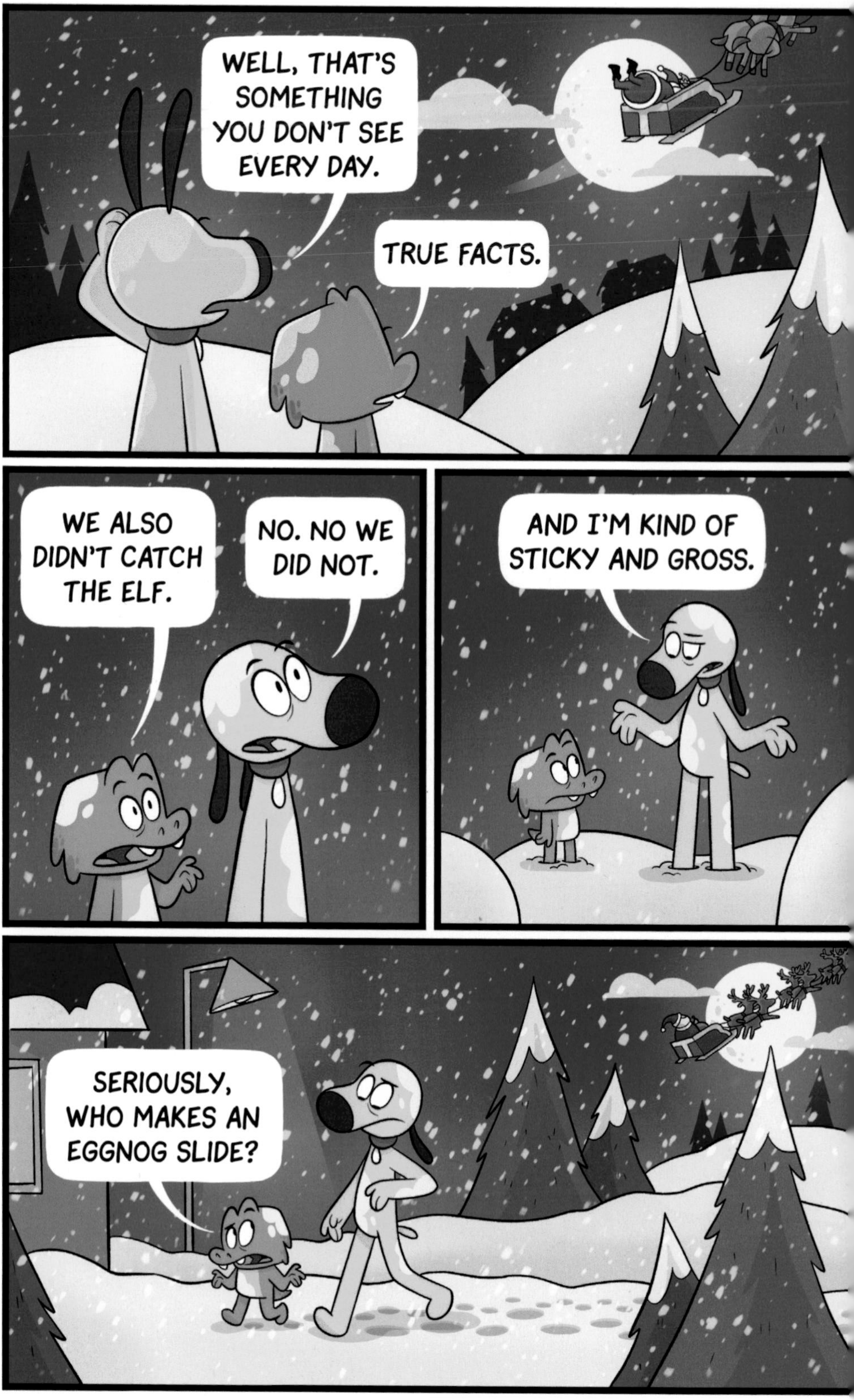
WELL, THAT'S SOMETHING YOU DON'T SEE EVERY DAY.
TRUE FACTS.
WE ALSO DIDN'T CATCH THE ELF.
NO. NO WE DID NOT.
AND I'M KIND OF STICKY AND GROSS.
SERIOUSLY, WHO MAKES AN EGGNOG SLIDE?

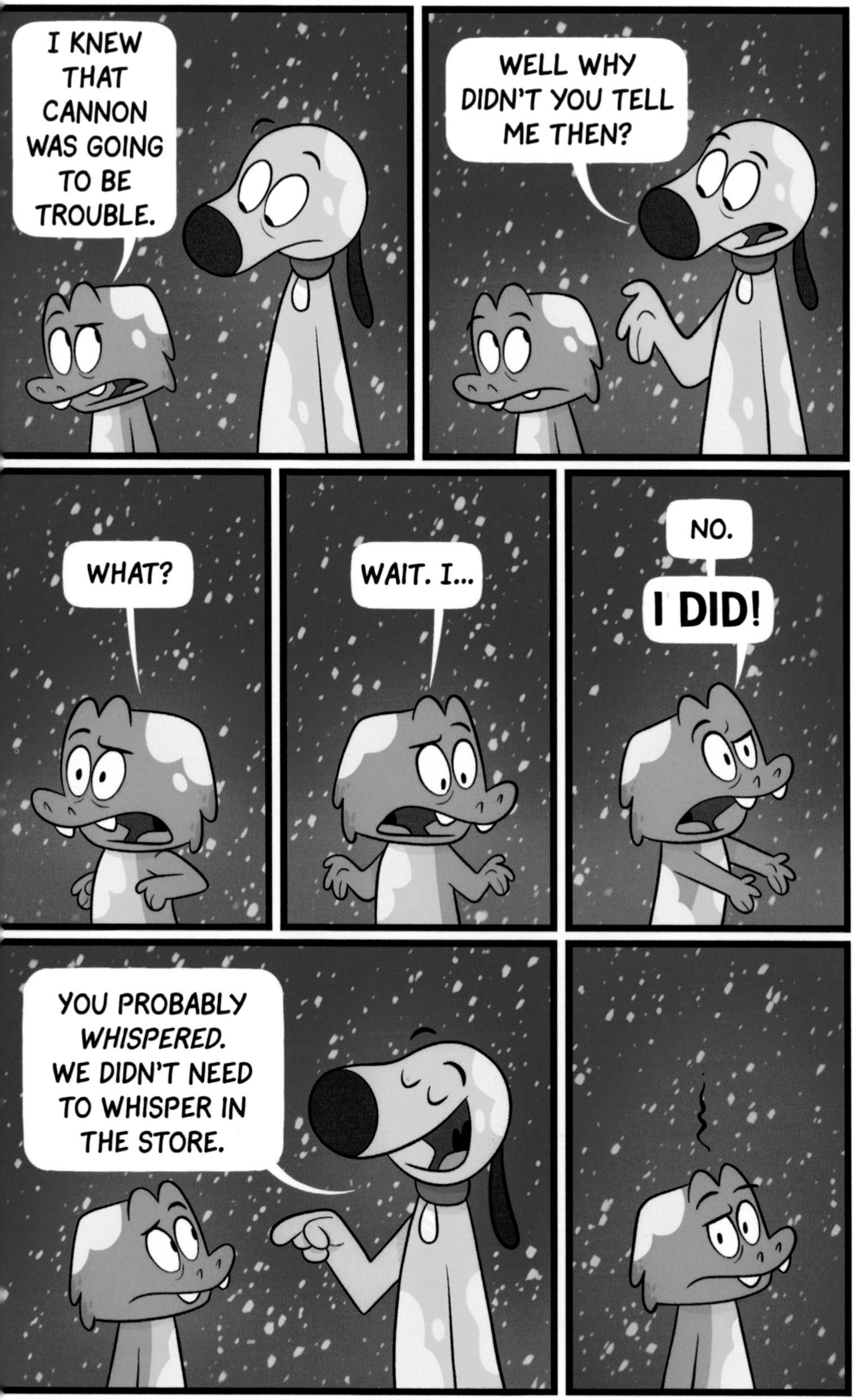
I KNEW THAT CANNON WAS GOING TO BE TROUBLE.
WELL WHY DIDN'T YOU TELL ME THEN?
WHAT?
WAIT. I...
NO.
I DID!
YOU PROBABLY *WHISPERED.* WE DIDN'T NEED TO WHISPER IN THE STORE.

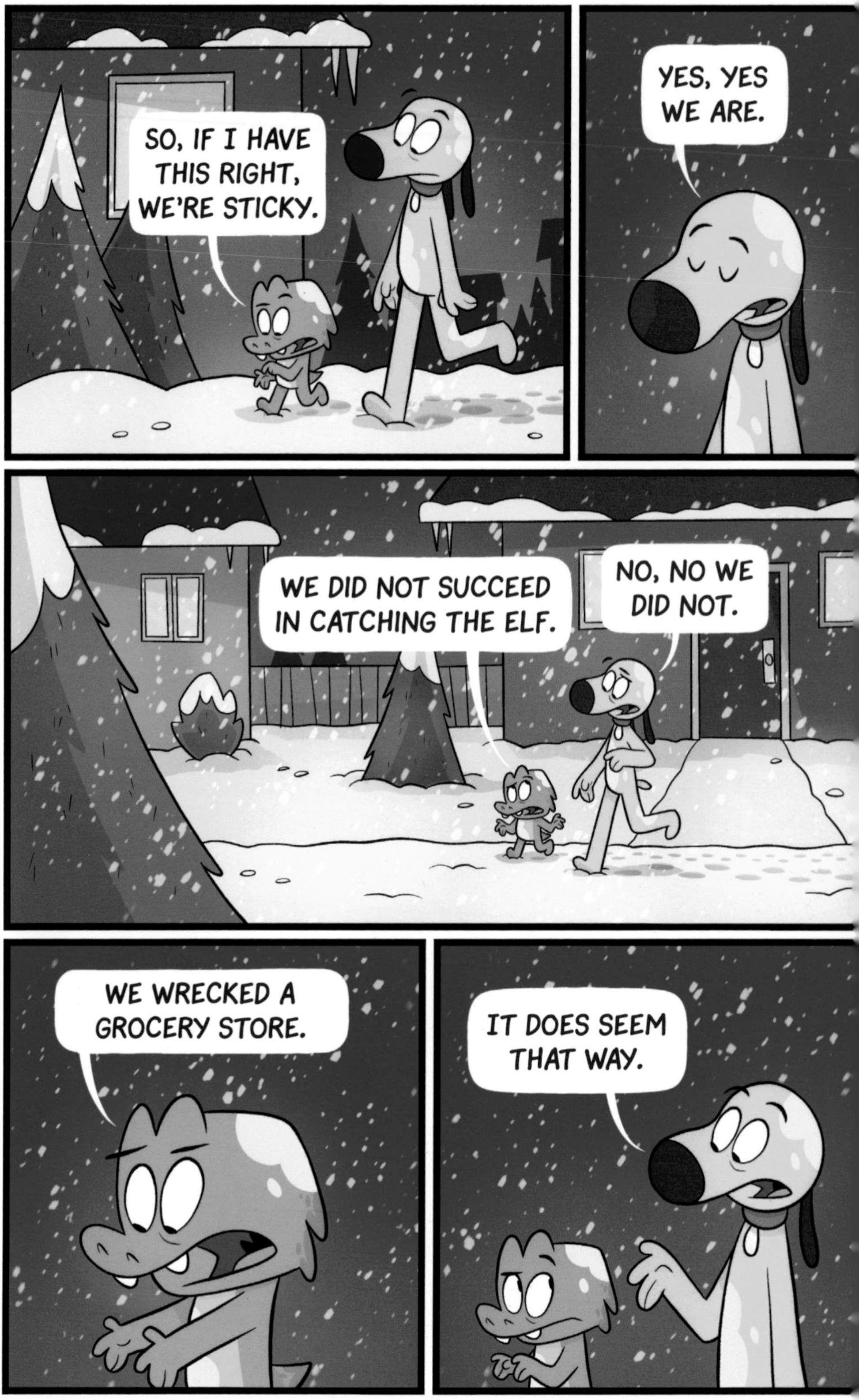

SO, IF I HAVE THIS RIGHT, WE'RE STICKY.
YES, YES WE ARE.
WE DID NOT SUCCEED IN CATCHING THE ELF.
NO, NO WE DID NOT.
WE WRECKED A GROCERY STORE.
IT DOES SEEM THAT WAY.

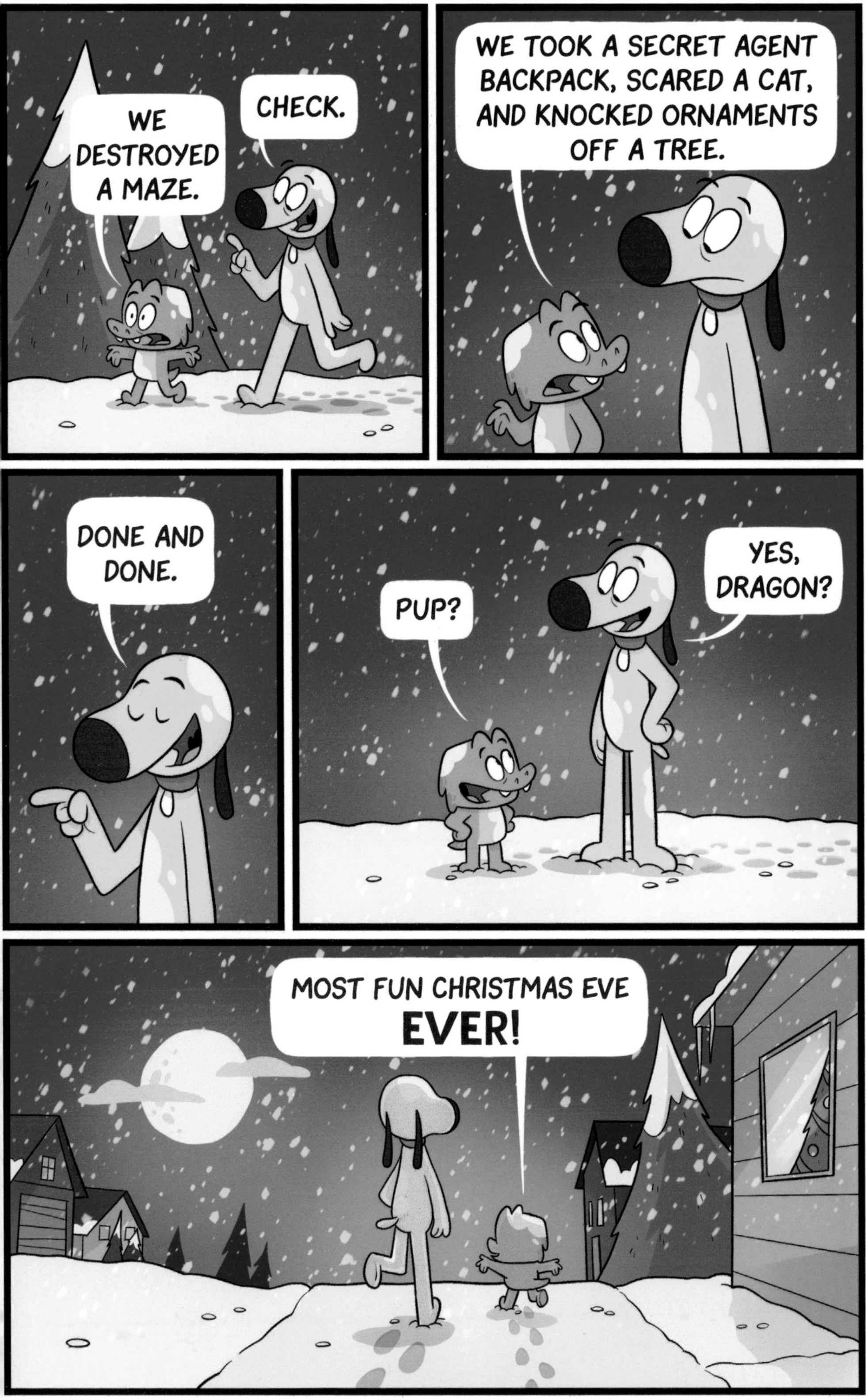
WE DESTROYED A MAZE.
CHECK.
WE TOOK A SECRET AGENT BACKPACK, SCARED A CAT, AND KNOCKED ORNAMENTS OFF A TREE.
DONE AND DONE.
PUP?
YES, DRAGON?
MOST FUN CHRISTMAS EVE **EVER!**

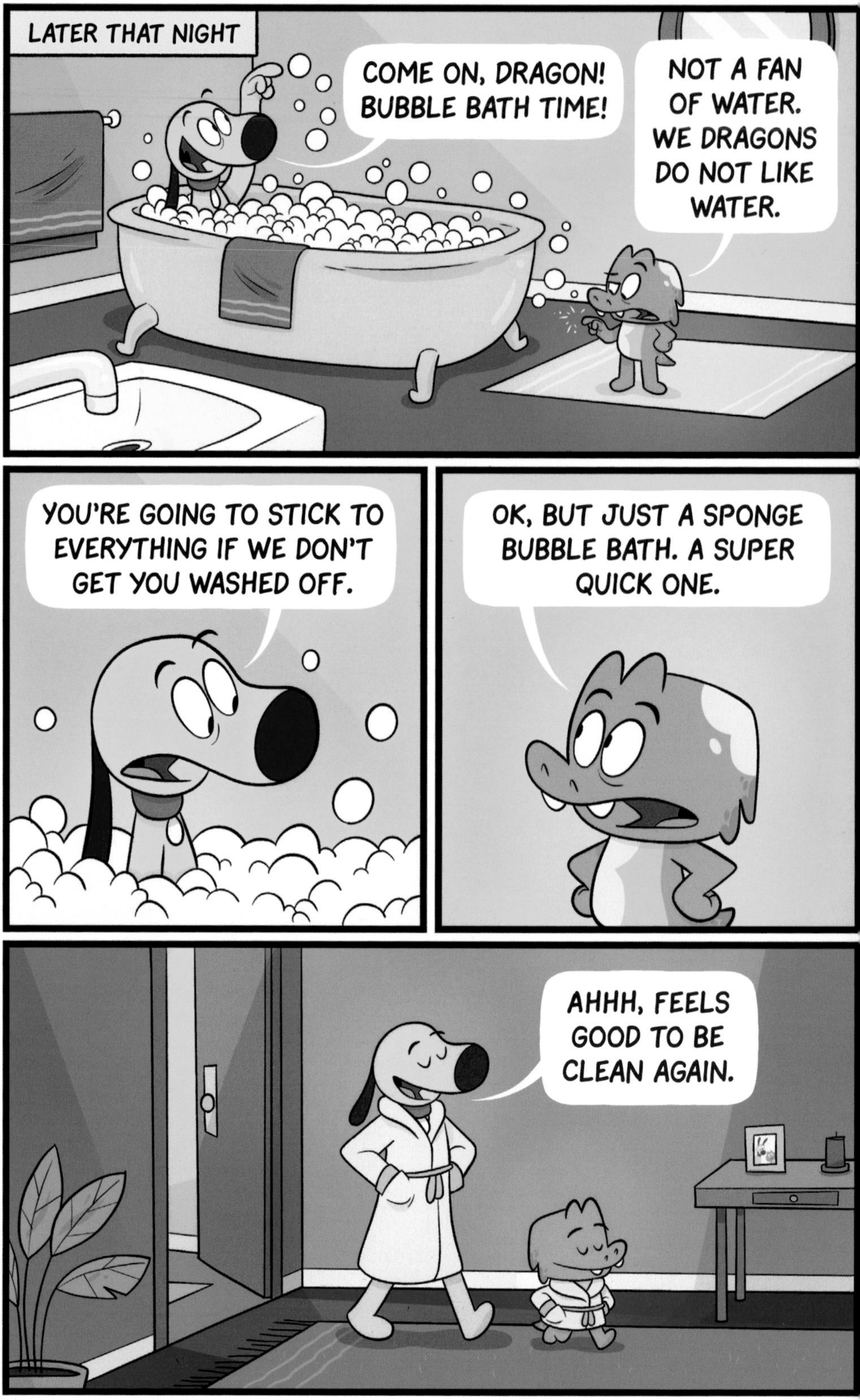
LATER THAT NIGHT
COME ON, DRAGON! BUBBLE BATH TIME!
NOT A FAN OF WATER. WE DRAGONS DO NOT LIKE WATER.
YOU'RE GOING TO STICK TO EVERYTHING IF WE DON'T GET YOU WASHED OFF.
OK, BUT JUST A SPONGE BUBBLE BATH. A SUPER QUICK ONE.
AHHH, FEELS GOOD TO BE CLEAN AGAIN.

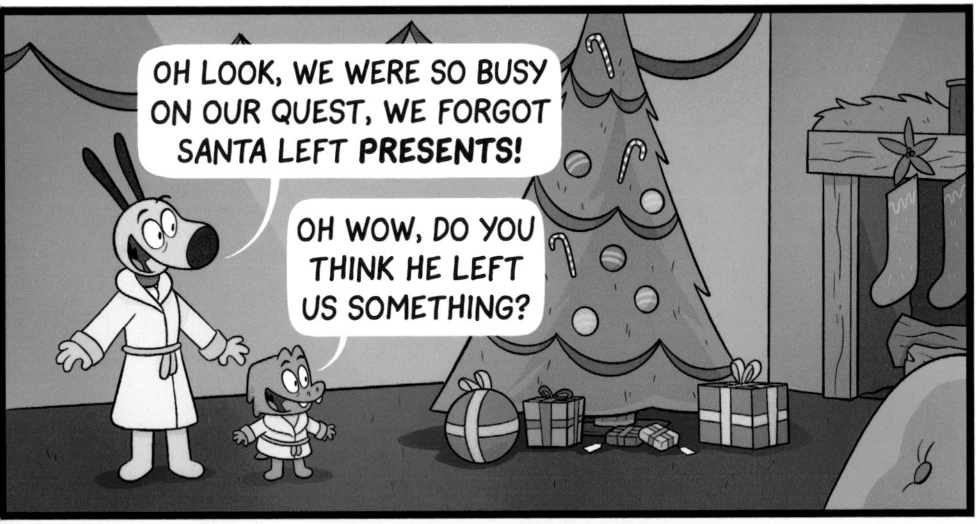
OH LOOK, WE WERE SO BUSY ON OUR QUEST, WE FORGOT SANTA LEFT **PRESENTS!**
OH WOW, DO YOU THINK HE LEFT US SOMETHING?

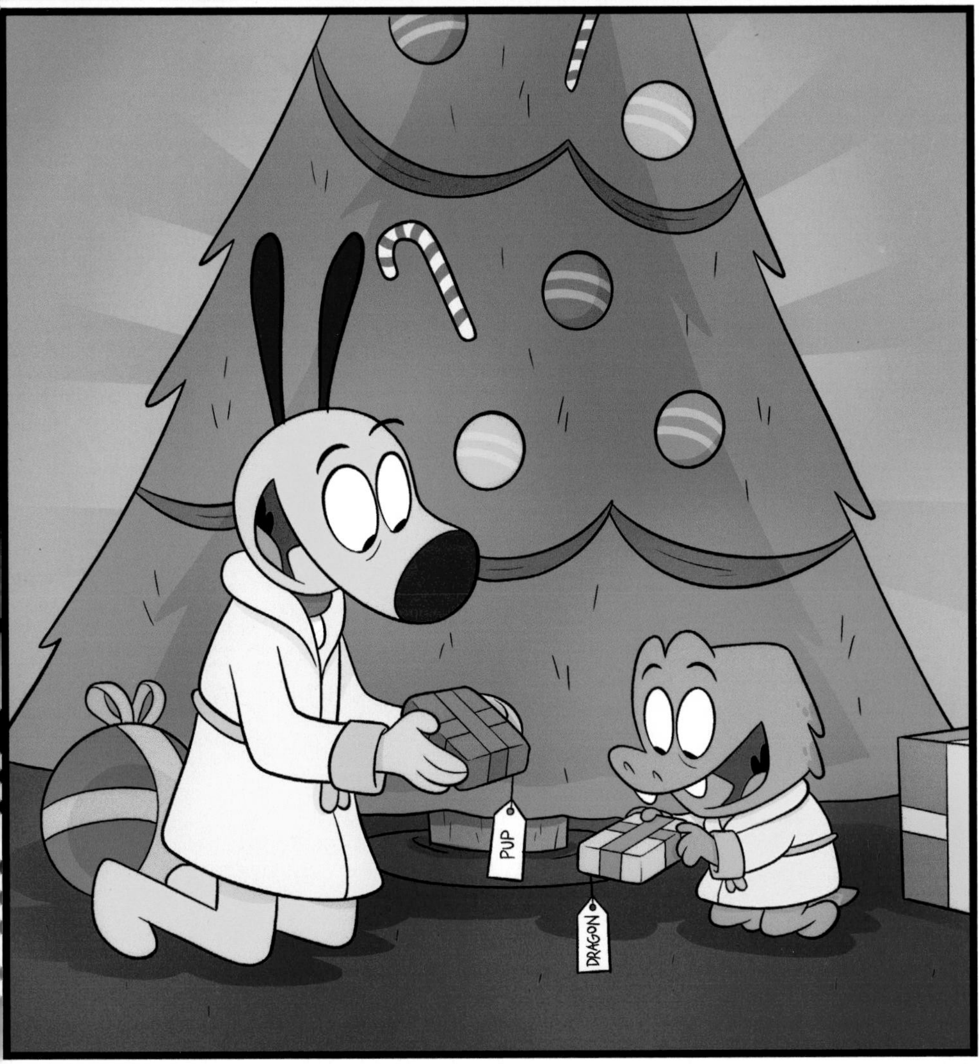
PUP
DRAGON

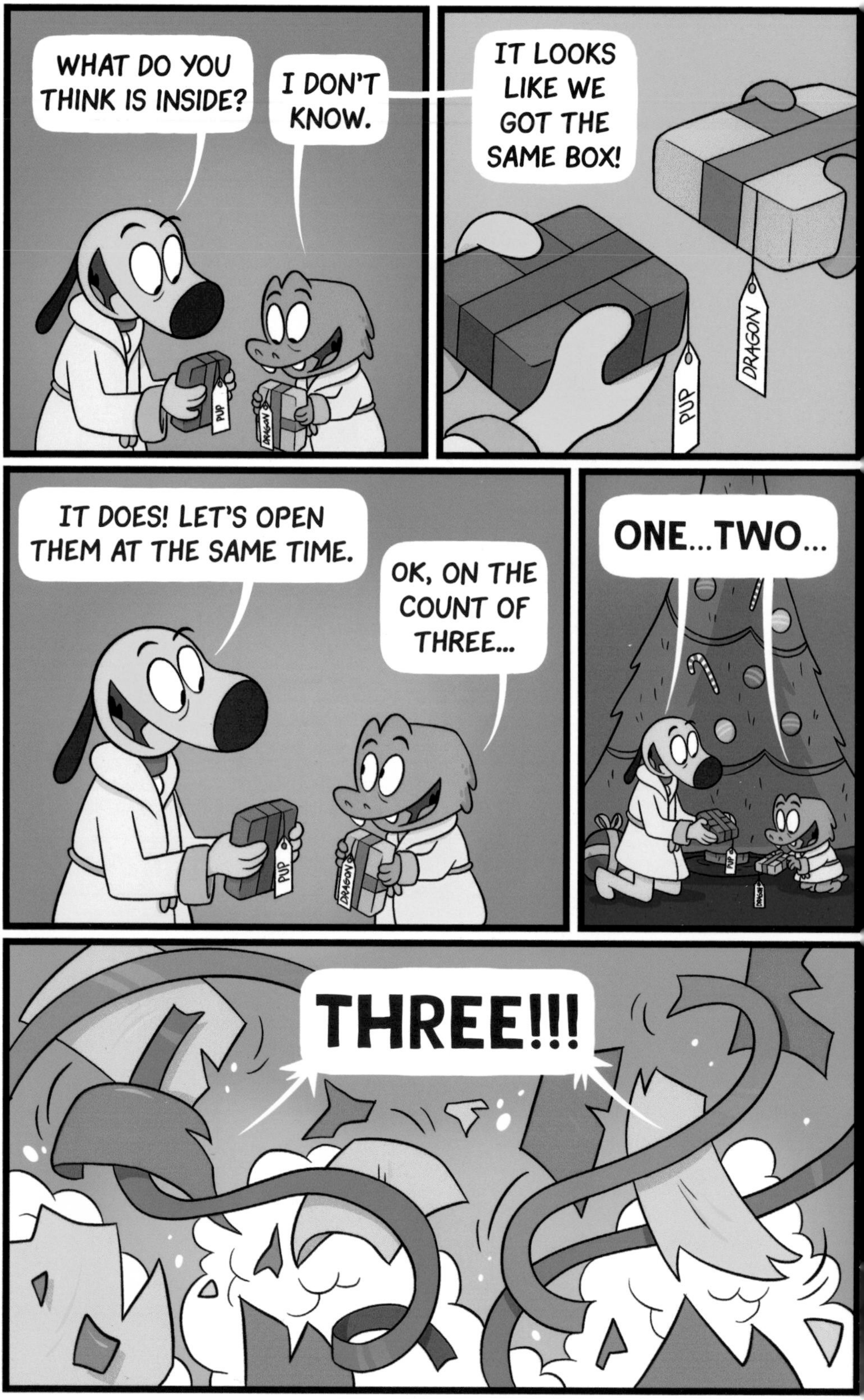
WHAT DO YOU THINK IS INSIDE?
I DON'T KNOW.
IT LOOKS LIKE WE GOT THE SAME BOX!
PUP
DRAGON
PUP
DRAGON
IT DOES! LET'S OPEN THEM AT THE SAME TIME.
OK, ON THE COUNT OF THREE...
PUP
DRAGON
ONE...TWO...
THREE!!!

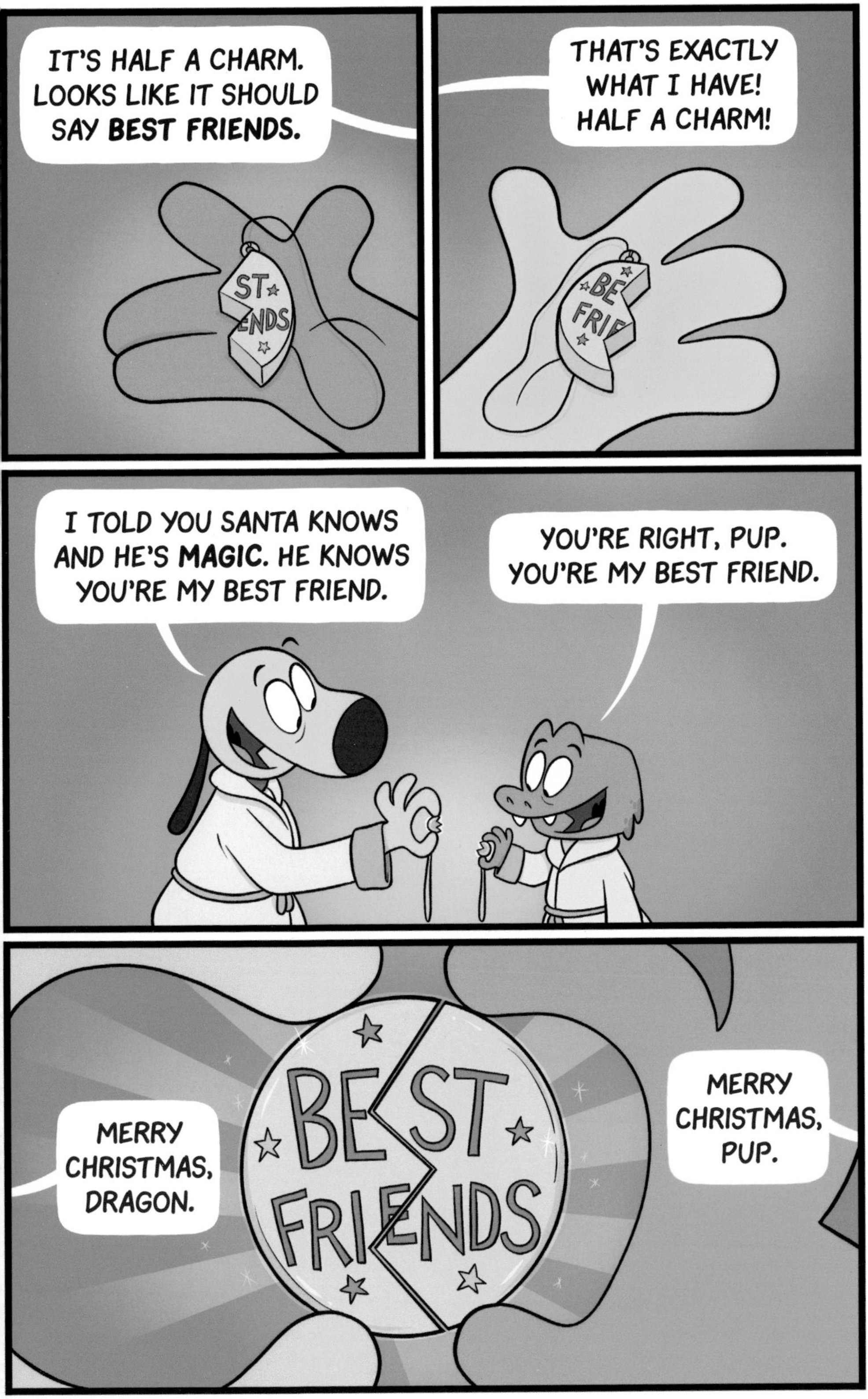
IT'S HALF A CHARM. LOOKS LIKE IT SHOULD SAY **BEST FRIENDS.**
ST ENDS
THAT'S EXACTLY WHAT I HAVE! HALF A CHARM!
BE FRI
I TOLD YOU SANTA KNOWS AND HE'S **MAGIC.** HE KNOWS YOU'RE MY BEST FRIEND.
YOU'RE RIGHT, PUP. YOU'RE MY BEST FRIEND.
BEST FRIENDS
MERRY CHRISTMAS, DRAGON.
MERRY CHRISTMAS, PUP.

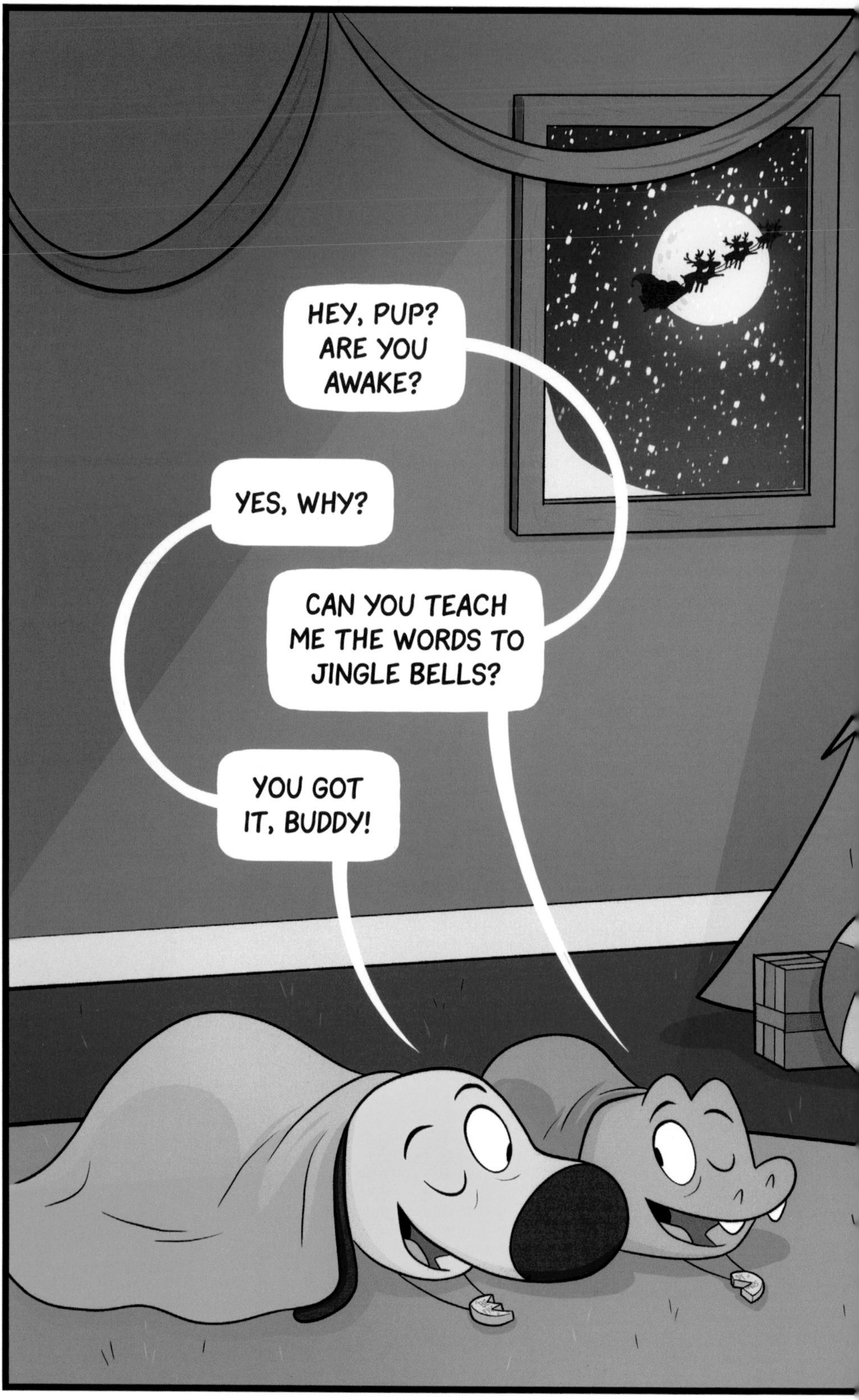
HEY, PUP? ARE YOU AWAKE?
YES, WHY?
CAN YOU TEACH ME THE WORDS TO JINGLE BELLS?
YOU GOT IT, BUDDY!

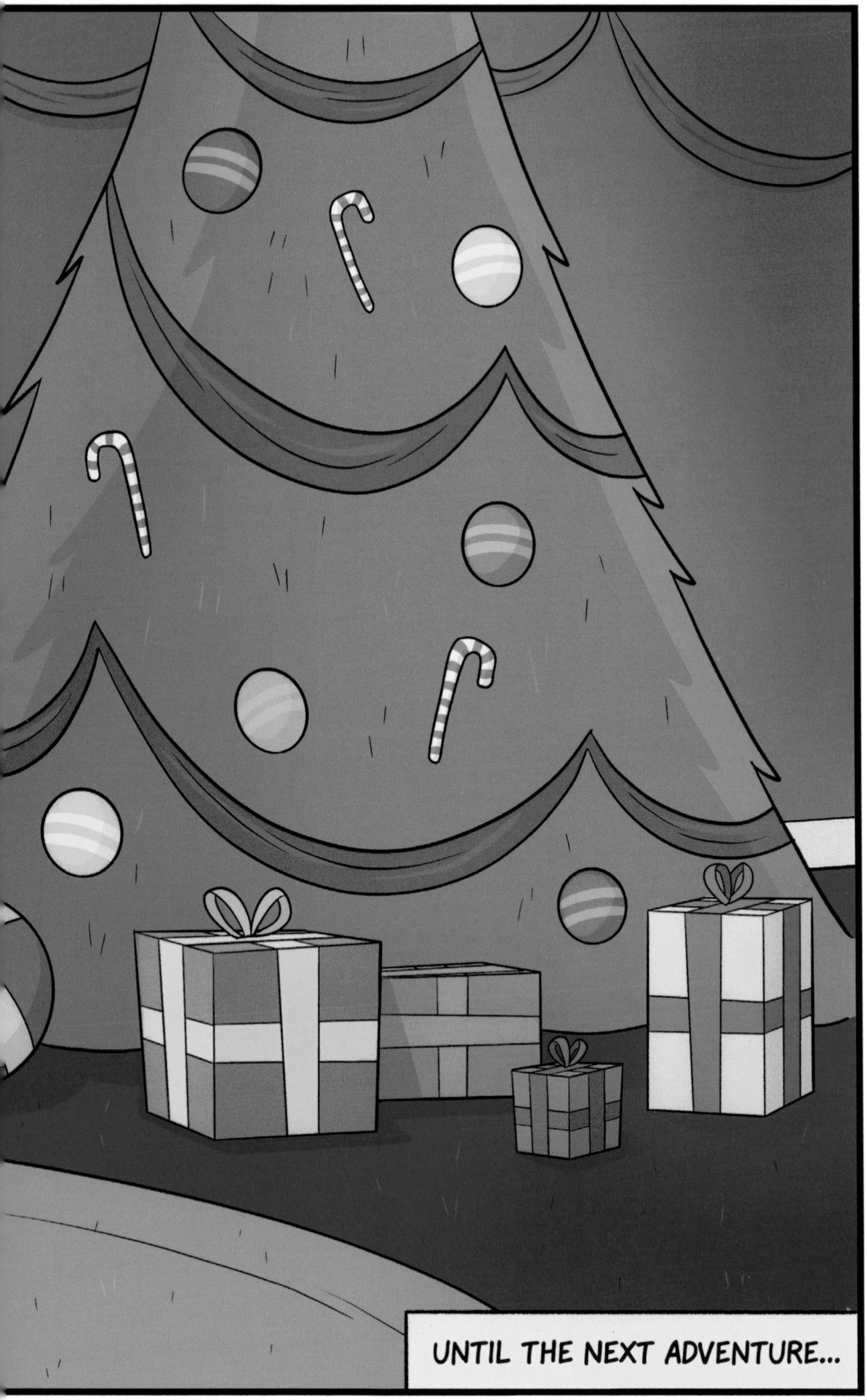
UNTIL THE NEXT ADVENTURE...

PUP AND DRAGON RETURN IN...

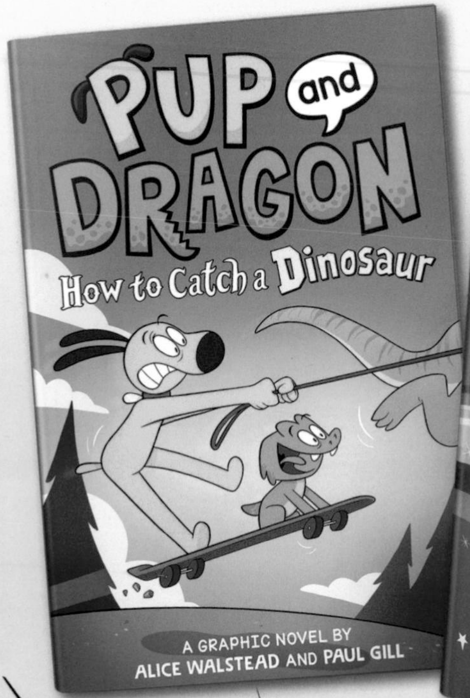
PUP and DRAGON
How to Catch a Dinosaur
A GRAPHIC NOVEL BY
ALICE WALSTEAD AND PAUL GILL

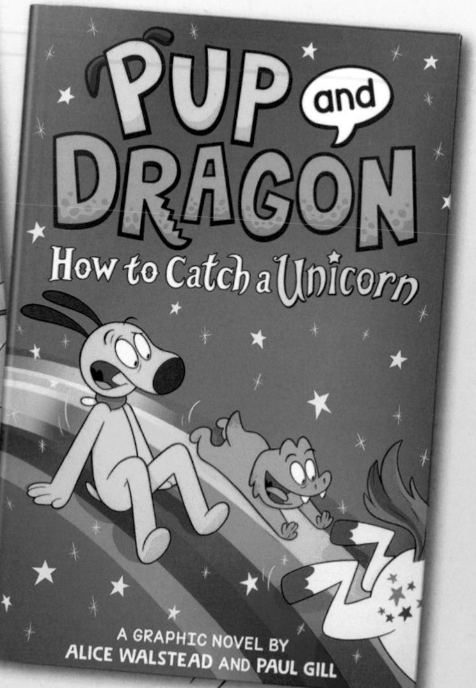
PUP and DRAGON
How to Catch a Unicorn
A GRAPHIC NOVEL BY
ALICE WALSTEAD AND PAUL GILL

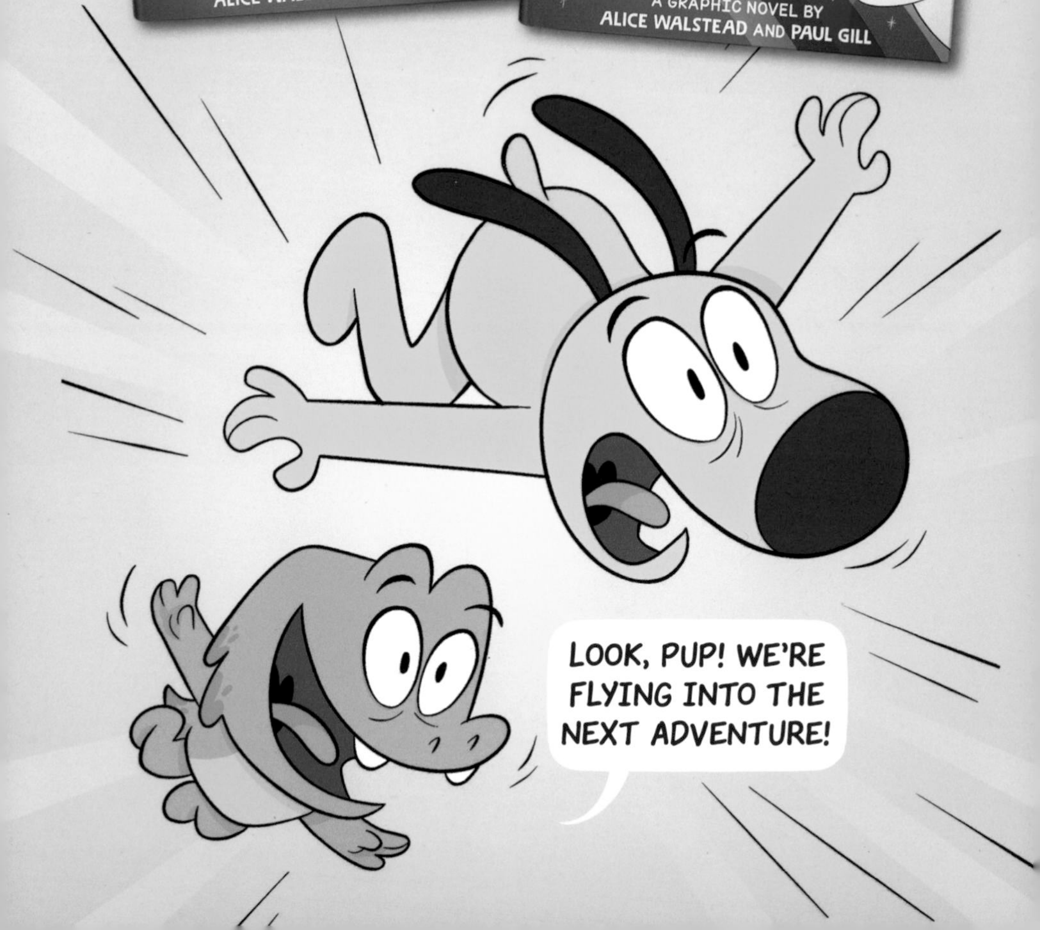
LOOK, PUP! WE'RE FLYING INTO THE NEXT ADVENTURE!

HOW TO DRAW
PUP and DRAGON

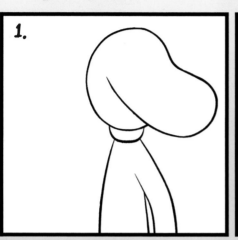

1.

1.

2.

2.

3.

3.

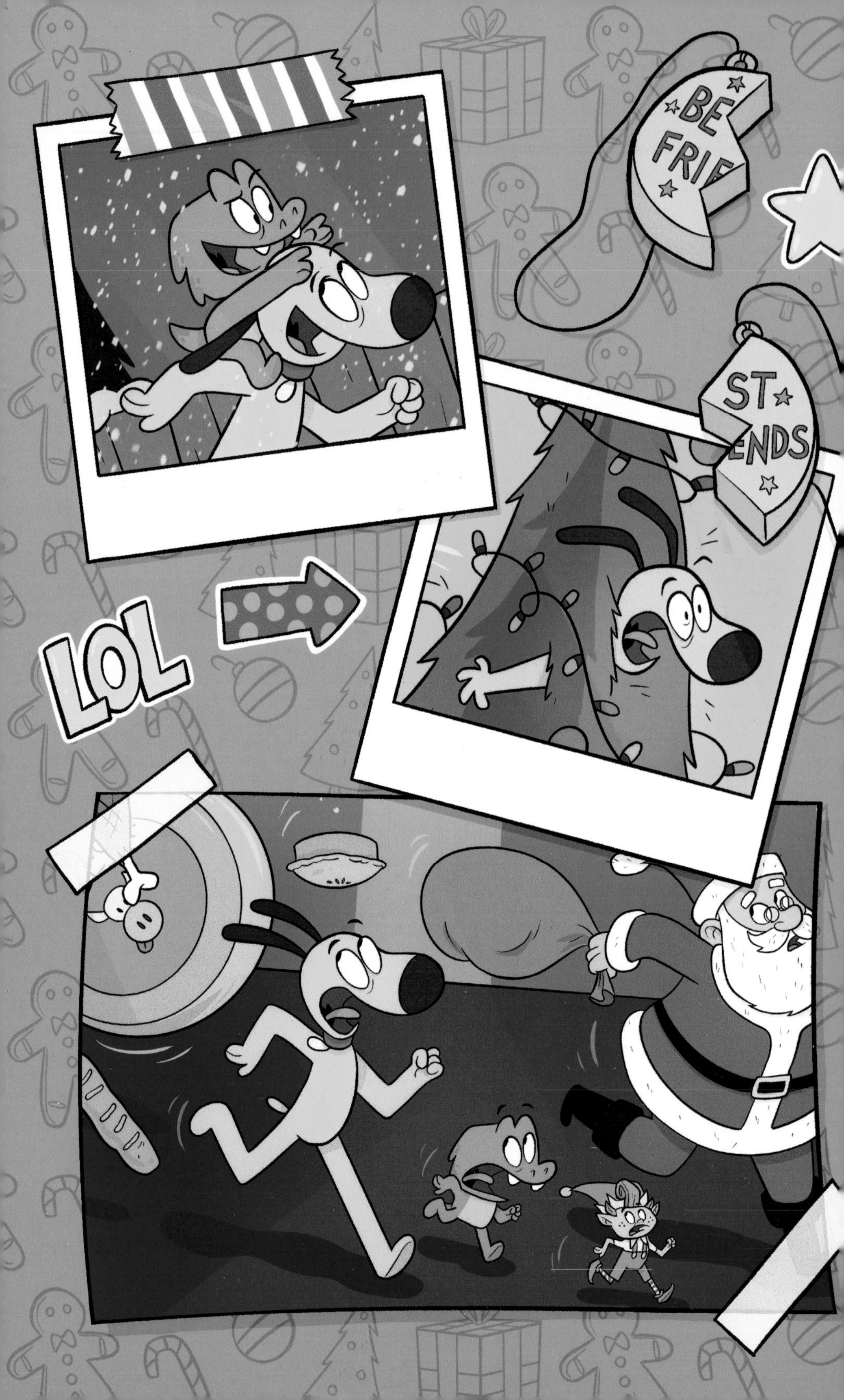
BE FRIE
ST ENDS
LOL